The Sterling Chronicles

Timothy Patrick Means

Mad Dog Press

The Sterling Chronicles
Copyright 2022 by Timothy Patrick Means

ISBN: 978-1-7376017-2-2
All rights reserved
Printed in the United States of America

No part of this book may be used or reproduced without the author's permission except for brief quotations embodied in critical articles and reviews.

This book is a work of fiction. Names, characters, places, and incidents are either a product of the author's imagination or are used fictitiously. Any resemblance to actual events, persons, or locales, living or dead, is purely coincidental.

Published by
Mad Dog Publications
Boise, Idaho

www.timothypatrickmeans .com

Cover design by sweetnspicydesigns.com

In a world both private and secure, everyday events continue to unfold. I'm referring to home life. There, meals are prepared, complete with homework and showers in the evening. I dedicate this book to my partner who makes all this possible: my wife, Janice. Without her hard work, none of this would have been possible, not the writing nor the time allotted me to create.

I bow to her love and devotion that keep this house running. And to you, my fans, a small voice now, but soon I suspect a crowd—all brought together to ask, "What's he thinking?"

Contents

Introduction 1

Chapter 1
Birth of a Paranormal 3

Chapter 2
A Child's Haunting 24

Chapter 3
Who Shot Robert Connelly? 58

Chapter 4
The Murder of April Humphry 86

Chapter 5
Achilles 97

Chapter 6
The Avenging Oath 107

Chapter 7
The Harmsworth Case 139

Acknowledgments 152

About the Author 153

Introduction

These pages are just a few exploits of Sterling, the mysterious psychic. One learns of his aptitudes and the struggles he faced throughout his life. The ability to see into the spiritual realm is a gift he both appreciated and despised because it not only often brought him closer to the living and the dead but also forced him to experience the last moments of the innocents whose lives had been cut short.

Sterling's relationships always seemed to fail due to his long absences or lack of intimacy, the results of shielding himself from those who got too close. His mother, a loveless woman, failed to raise him in a supportive, loving environment. She, the unfaithful wife, mostly caroused the bars in search of anyone who could satisfy her cravings and lust—even for just one night.

At the end of her life, death was the only thing they shared; that fateful night, so many years ago, his life hung in the balance. Sterling was spared certain death; instead, he was given a gift that became a heavy burden.

All alone with his unique abilities to search the last known whereabouts of the dearly departed, the man has become simply Sterling.

Immune to love or any other senseless emotion, his mission in life was to discover the facts—no matter how painful the truth was to the families.

Chapter 1
Birth of a Paranormal

STERLING SAW FLASHING lights ahead. A highway patrolman was directing traffic around a collision on the right side of the highway, cloaked in shadowy darkness. As Sterling inched forward, he could see a station wagon and a pickup entwined in a tangled wreck of metal and broken glass. Both vehicles' engine compartments were still smoking, sending a steam plume into the air. As he got closer, he noticed a fireman applying fire retardant to both cars. Nearby, small children huddled together as their mother was taken off on a stretcher. The truck owner hadn't fared even that well; his body hung halfway out of his windshield—no doubt the result of not wearing his seat belt—and a tarp was covering his remains.

Sterling flashed back to a similar crash. When he was that child on the side of the road, the same type of tarp was placed over his mother's body. It was the end of a chapter of his life, and when he looked back, he did not regret that he had been left an orphan at a young age. His birth had been regretted by both his mother and father. Even to a child of tender years, it became painfully apparent that his mother loved neither him nor his father. She could not find happiness with her husband; she could not find happiness as a mother. Instead, she chose to search for it in the arms of another man.

As he drove past the accident, pitying the children whose lives had just been so tragically altered, his mind wandered back to his own childhood.

IT WAS ON A FRIGIDLY COLD night. He and his father had driven around town for what seemed like hours looking for his mother. They'd finally found her in an old honky-tonk off the interstate. She, of course, was drunk, dancing with her arms around another man. His father, a tall man no one would tangle with, angrily demanded she return home.

Sterling drove home with his parents, staring out the frosted back windows of the car. His father, somewhat distracted, could only stare at the passenger seat with disgust, shaking his head. His mother, Emma-Jean, was oblivious to his hateful stares and rested in a drunken stupor against the cold window glass.

The highway was slick and frozen. Sterling's father struggled to keep the car in his lane; maybe it would have been wiser of him to drive the slower roads through town rather than take the main interstate. But, in all fairness, the young boy knew, after the incident in the bar, his father wasn't thinking straight.

Nervously, Sterling sat in the back seat and prayed for them to make it home safely. But what he feared most was not an accident but the fighting and arguing that would erupt when they did arrive—the bitter quarreling of two unhappy people no longer in love. He never understood their reasons for staying together, but whatever misery they felt toward one another ended that cold December evening back in 1961.

Suddenly, their car hit an icy patch in the road and

skidded into the oncoming lane toward a diesel truck carrying decorative iron fences, the pilings stacked high above the cab. As the trucker locked his brakes, the semi jackknifed, causing the heavy load to break apart, sending sharp iron spikes toward the car, and impaling both his father and mother—killing them instantly. In the back seat Sterling was only slightly luckier. The pipe piercing his mother's body pushed through the car seat and lodged into Sterling's chest.

He, too, would have died instantly if the force of the spike had not been slowed as it penetrated his mother. Now, so many years later, Sterling grabbed his chest, feeling once again the piercing pain. That night everything changed. Somehow he became something different. As he was dying, impaled on the fence post, he felt his soul connect to his mother's as if they were one. The world outside the car faded away. No longer could he sense the icy wind blowing through the shattered windshield nor see the trees, lifeless and bare from the winter storm. Although pinned to the back of her seat, he could see his mother, knowing it wasn't her physical body that he saw. Instead, it was her soul. It left her body, floated above him, gave him one last sorrowful look, and began its journey to the other side.

Sterling waited impatiently to be released from his earthly body, and the excruciating pain was so great that he could not even breathe enough to scream his agony. He began to see the world around him change and become unfocused. The pain in his body was fading, and he welcomed death happily. He expected to follow his mother soon—it didn't matter that she had never loved him; she was the only mother he had. Without her and his father, he was alone. He wanted to follow but could not.

Sterling lay in the car bleeding, at the edge of death, when a young police officer arrived at the scene. Only a few months on the job, Jack Danbury was horrified at the sight of this young boy, blood flowing out of him as if from a fountain. He wanted to save him. Desperately, he called for assistance and put pressure on the wound to stop the bleeding until an ambulance could arrive.

Sterling stared at the man, searching for answers. The stranger held his hand tightly, whispering words of comfort that Sterling could barely hear as his life force faded. Sterling felt a sense of relief; all his sadness and disappointment were ending. It no longer mattered; a peaceful, calm, and loving feeling overcame him.

Somehow, through the haze and through his yearning to follow his mother as quickly as he could, the words of the nervous policeman reached him: "Everything is going to be all right...help is coming...hang in there, kid."

Sterling tried to ignore the words. He tried to let go. Still, Officer Danbury would not give up. He kept the pressure on his wound, somehow keeping him bound to his body.

At the time this annoyed Sterling greatly. He kept asking himself, "Why won't he let me go?" All he wanted was to travel into the great afterlife.

Strangers tugged at his lifeless body. He was pulled free of the car. He wanted to cry out but could make no sound. He knew he was being lifted in the air. Someone poked his arm with a needle. Sterling felt the cold on his skin as his coat and shirt were ripped off his body. Something was laid across his chest, and he was hurriedly shoved into a vehicle. Doors slammed behind him, and a single siren screamed out noisily as it drove quickly away. Sleep overtook him in a way that he could not resist, and the next thing he remembered he was waking up in a hospital, all alone, wrapped in bandages that covered his chest, the pain overwhelming.

THREE WEEKS LATER Sterling was finally let out of the

hospital. He had nowhere else to go. His Uncle Steve, a happy bachelor, took him in. Steve was no father image; over the years he was often left alone to fend for himself.

After some time he became friends with a kid down the block, Joshua, and they soon began getting into trouble together. Truth be told, Sterling led Joshua astray, not the other way around. Sterling had nothing to do after school and no reason not to get into mischief. Nothing big—at first. But Joshua's father, a senior karate instructor, heard about it and asked Uncle Steve for permission to bring Sterling with him to Joshua's karate classes and teach him some discipline.

Sterling was excited. It would be great to learn how to kick and punch. However, he never realized that Joshua's father, Master Jeremiah Koji, tolerated nothing but pure dedication to his art. Yes, Sterling learned to kick and punch, and he also found a man to look up to in his life. He wanted to be the best for Master Jeremiah. Sterling didn't realize it at the time but he had found his niche in life. He became Master Jeremiah's best student, even better than Joshua, his son, who was more interested in girls than learning to break wood with his bare hands.

AS STERLING LEFT the accident behind, turned off the interstate, and drove to his home, he thought, *Of course, I could have carried on the traditions of martial arts, but what Master Jeremiah didn't realize was all that training was honing another ability.*

The divination that began when he connected to his dying mother grew more vigorous. It could not be ignored. The discipline he learned, both physical and mental, as he practiced karate, unconsciously at first, helped him to train his psychic abilities.

He didn't know it then but soon he would need to tap into that energy to help find someone close to him. This gift of cognitive abilities was both a blessing and a curse.

Sterling struggled in his friendships with both guys and girls as a teenager. His good looks, wit, and humor made him popular with everyone at school, but he always knew when someone lied. It made it difficult to get close to anyone—particularly teenage girls, whom Sterling discovered at an early age, who exaggerated and pretended and downright lied anytime they wanted to impress him; if they'd only known, this just turned Sterling off. And for that very reason his psychic abilities kept him from making close friends.

Throughout his childhood he felt guilty that he hadn't done more to make his father aware of the winter conditions on the roads. His parents had been so busy arguing that his father had paid no attention to the weather. But even before they headed out to find his mother, Sterling had had a hunch that something horrible would happen. He didn't know it then but it was his first psychic experience.

He knew they should stay home. He timidly suggested it to his father but the man refused to listen. As the years went by, it would happen again. Not often, just sometimes. He would have nothing but a substantial feeling, just a suspicion that something terrible would happen to someone, and the closer he was to the person, the stronger the feeling. But how do you tell a close friend that something terrible is about to happen? How do you explain that? When he tried he was laughed at, his premonitions excused as nonsense or, worse for a young man, seen as cowardice.

As he grew older he chose a solitary life; it was better than seeing those he cared for suddenly have a tragedy befall them—easily avoidable if only they would have listened to him. The pressure he felt when he had a premonition was maddening, and it only worsened when he tried to warn someone. He would ask a friend not to travel here or there, not to go hunting, not to go out with that girl. And they laughed at him and his suggestions. The alternative was better in the end. He simply built a wall between the world and himself.

THERE WAS ONLY ONE PERSON he let inside that wall. Jack Danbury, the relentless guardian angel, the young police officer who saved his life in the accident that killed his parents, would often call to ensure he stayed out of trouble. Never far away, Jack became more like an uncle than a police officer—more of an uncle, in fact, than Uncle Steve, his legal guardian. Sterling and Jack often attended an afternoon baseball game, enjoying the ballpark franks or salted peanuts. So, at age seventeen, Sterling had many acquaintances but few friends. He was well-liked in school but known as a loner, his real focus on his martial arts training.

And then he met Charlotte Ann Kemp, who often picked up her younger brother John after his martial arts lessons at the Dojo. John, just age fifteen, was being bullied in school; he had come to the Dojo to learn how to defend himself. He no longer wanted to be seen as small and weak. Charlotte appreciated the help Sterling gave John, and after appearing several times at the Dojo, a friendship began, then it only grew closer. There was something different about Charlotte that Sterling found attractive. Not only was she kind and intelligent but she was also determined to get what she wanted; what she wanted was him.

Thinking back to that terrible day, he remembered she had disappeared three days after her seventeenth birthday. On the night of her disappearance, Charlotte drove the family car to the Dojo to pick up John. That evening Sterling's master had a pressing engagement, allowing him to teach in his absence.

As Charlotte waited for her brother in the parking lot, something in Sterling's spirit distracted him and made it difficult to concentrate. Suddenly, the feeling of lightheadedness overcame him. He felt as if he was drunk.

As he closed his eyes, images of a girl screaming for help echoed in his subconscious. It overwhelmed him. He felt faint, dizzy. He thought he was going to collapse.

Needing a second to gather his senses, he told the class that the lessons were over, and they collected their things. Thankfully, the parents had already begun arriving to pick up their kids. He tried to avoid them; he didn't want to freak out anyone by his strange behavior.

Once the students were gone, Sterling turned to John and asked, "I wonder why Charlotte hasn't come inside the Dojo. Look, you can still see the headlights turned on. Come on; I'll walk you out to the car."

When they arrived at the family car, it was empty. Fear and panic overcame them both. Sterling screamed out Charlotte's name but heard no reply.

A minute later, without warning, a distant scream flooded Sterling's spiritual senses, and he struggled to stand. Looking over at John, he yelled, "Quickly, search the area for Charlotte—she's close by. And John, prepare yourself for battle. If someone has her and you encounter them, remember all your training. Fight. Fight and kill, if you must, but run now and find Charlotte!"

As John disappeared, calling Charlotte's name, Sterling searched for her in another way as he sat on the ground next to the empty car. Closing his eyes, he concentrated on the silence of the night, nothing but the blackness of the two worlds, with no light around him. He tried his best to control his breathing and attune himself to the two worlds. One world was physical, and the other spiritual. But he couldn't concentrate; instead, he saw the endless blackness of the night. His thoughts drifted to the images of the past and wouldn't cooperate.

Angry at himself, he screamed out in frustration, hitting the ground with his fist and causing his heart rate to quicken instead of slowing down.

"Why is this happening? Why has this gift of connecting the two worlds failed me when I need it the most? What good is it if it doesn't work when you want it the most?" he screamed aloud, again hitting the ground and losing control.

Control was always a fundamental principle in the teachings that he had instructed others in. The martial arts were designed to control one's anger and breathing. *Yes, essential breathing. I can't reach the other world in a fit of rage.* The adrenaline coursing through his body wouldn't allow him to relax; instead, his body seemed prepared for battle, not meditation. The simple truth was he needed to regain his tranquility and understanding of the true nature of reality and one's place in it. There, in that place, he could harness the invisible power of Chi.

Slowly, he attempted to relax his body to control his breathing while panicking inside. The screams that he'd heard in his psyche were now silent. "Why, oh why, was this happening to Charlotte, sweet Charlotte?" he whispered to himself while regulating his physical body. But as his tears ran down his face, he knew the silence meant one thing: death.

IN HIS QUIET APARTMENT, reliving that memory brought back all the hurt and frustration he'd experienced that day. Back then he'd tried his best to get control of the situation, screaming out the word, "Obey." He chanted that one word repeatedly while his eyes remained closed to outside influences. He couldn't say how long he was there on the ground, repeating "obey," but soon his surroundings changed, and he could see through the darkness—a colorful spectrum of light appeared in front of him as his heart rhythms continued to slow.

The sounds of the city faded and grew muffled. Suddenly, he saw an eerie world of different shapes, buildings, and houses next to a road decorated in red. That's where he felt closest to Charlotte's essence. Her spiritual aura of luminous radiance surrounded her being like a halo of bright colors.

He saw a solitary pickup driving down the highway. In the driver's seat sat a bearded man. As he floated above the vehicle, he saw an old, faded green tarp covering a small mound; junk was placed over it. Then he saw a frightening sight: a glimpse of Charlotte's spirit holding her hands to him. She begged him for rescue.

Immediately, he understood. Charlotte wasn't dead yet as he had feared. She was just unconscious. Her limp body under the old, tattered tarp was soon to become a sacrificial offering for the morbid desires of this sick-minded monster. Desperately, Sterling looked for details about the truck: its license plate number or other discernable sign of whom it belonged. He recognized it as a 1959 Chevrolet stepside. At the back bumper he could barely make out the number 37.

The truck itself looked old, with rust stains and crumpled fenders. Sterling quickly stared at the driver to see his face and struggled to draw closer, wanting to see him and know this fiend that had taken Charlotte. As his senses drew him closer, more details of the face began to emerge; sunken cheekbones and bulging eyes were all visible. The man wore a simple old baseball cap that hid his complete identity. Regardless, there was something upon his neck—yes, a tattoo of a thick chain around his neck that crossed through a skull, opening its mouth and displaying a missing tooth. The tattoo was in the center of the throat, covering his Adam's apple. Sterling drew closer, studying him.

Suddenly, out of nowhere, a distant voice yelled out from the other world, breaking his concentration. Opening his eyes, there standing next to him was a disappointed John announcing, "I can't find Charlotte anywhere."

"We have to call the police," Sterling said urgently.

Racing back to the Dojo, he called Jack Danbury. When

Jack arrived at the Dojo, Sterling hysterically explained that Charlotte had been kidnapped. Jack put out an all-points bulletin after hearing about the precise details of the truck, the two numbers in the license place, and the abductor's features.

John quickly notified his parents. They arrived, frantic to know what had happened to their daughter. Sterling didn't want to say anything except what was evident to everyone: Someone had taken Charlotte but he didn't know who or why.

Sterling had never confided about his abilities to anyone—not even Jack. That part of him was a secret. It wasn't that he couldn't trust Jack with the truth of his ability to connect with the spiritual world. He could tell Jack anything—anything but that. Jack was a hardened cop. He'd started working in skid row and other derelict parts of the city where life was cheap and could be bought or sold for a price. Jack made a name for himself on those hardened streets as a tough-as-nails cop.

And Sterling knew that.

Jack only believed in facts; he could never comprehend the hidden spiritual world surrounding us. He never suspected that the boy whose life he saved could see into the supernatural life force realm or be able to travel into time in search of clues—a gift he would hew to a fine point in search of his one true love.

Sterling sat alone remembering, and a tear ran down his cheek. He quickly wiped it away. After all these years the pain of losing Charlotte still haunted him, an open wound that only festered. It defined him as the solitary tall, dark stranger who saw visions of another world where loved ones traveled before reaching their final destination.

After Charlotte went missing, sleep evaded Sterling for days; he refused to eat anything but some steamed vegetables and water, leaving him weak and barely able to move. He searched the transcendent realm for Charlotte's whereabouts in his spirit and came away with nothing. He decided he would have better luck contacting Charlotte if he visited her family.

He spent several hours with them. When it grew late Charlotte's mom invited him to stay the night in Charlotte's bedroom: *He looked too tired and ill,* she thought, *to send him out late at night.* Outside a storm appeared from the south, and the rain became steadily more violent with each passing hour.

As Sterling slept in Charlotte's bedroom, all his spiritual faculties were focused on the girl. Perhaps his body was suffering from malnourishment or his lack of desire to continue living in this cruel world left him in a weakened state. Still, he soon would have to surrender to his physical needs, regardless of how much he wanted to leave this world behind by starving himself.

Sterling stared up at Charlotte's graduation photo, the pretty, young girl who had stolen his heart, as he sat in her room alone. *If only I could close my eyes and picture Charlotte, perhaps her whereabouts would suddenly reveal themselves.* He felt Charlotte's spirit in the room with him.

Overly tired, he fell asleep, and everything around him changed. His spirit journeyed between the two worlds. Because of his weakened body, the other dimension was sharper than he had ever seen it before. He searched for any sign of Charlotte and found himself high in the clouds, looking down at the city below. He saw the world around him as something ugly and cold. Staring down, he saw an image of a couple screaming at one another in their apartment. The husband reached into his coat, took out a gun, and shot his wife in the head, killing her instantly. Then he turned the gun on himself and fired.

Another scene appeared. A prostitute was tortured, strapped to a bed. The monster began to cut her while her muffled screams were barely audible over the gag in her mouth.

The vision changed again. Sterling saw an old blue house in a forgotten neighborhood near a railroad spur in the south part of town. There, in the garage, he saw Charlotte—still alive.

In Sterling's vision, he could see Charlotte struggle to get free as she lay naked on a table. Wrapped around her were thick chains that held her into place. She was wearing a gag in her mouth and jerked her body side to side but could not free herself.

The shadowy figure walked up next to her, holding a rubber hose in his hands. He lifted her head and wrapped the tube tightly around her neck. Then, taking the two ends of the hose, he gripped it tightly and began to strangle Charlotte. She kicked her legs madly side to side to get free but soon the kicking stopped, and she remained motionless.

Sterling, sitting in her bedroom, was helpless to interfere. His shouts had no effect. He screamed Charlotte's name but the murdering bastard, far away in the unknown garage, could not hear Sterling.

Sterling helplessly watched as, sometime later, the man freed her lifeless body from the chains that bound her; he watched as the murderer took Charlotte's body out to the backyard and deposited it in a shallow grave. He covered her up with dirt and, as an afterthought, the son of a bitch stomped on her grave until he was sure the ground was packed. Soon after the murderer planted some red flowers on top of it. Then, having completed his deed, he returned to the house as if nothing had happened.

Sterling was sick to his stomach. Nausea awoke him from his vision, and he returned to the physical reality of Charlotte's bedroom. He ran to the bathroom and vomited in the toilet, then called Jack who agreed to come over to Sterling's home as soon as he could make his excuses and leave Charlotte's parents.

Early the following day Sterling and Jack sat together in his uncle's kitchen. Jack listened silently, only raising an eyebrow a few times as Sterling explained first his powers—for he had never mentioned them before—and then exactly what he had seen. Sterling could describe every detail of the man who had kidnapped Charlotte: his description, the truck he drove, the type of house the man owned.

Jack was a skeptic. He had never believed in visions or spirits or premonitions. How could Sterling know these things? But seeing the young man he cared for in such a dreadful state, he thought humoring might help him. Jack decided to assist in any way he could.

Working together as a team, Sterling and Jack soon combed the south side, intently exploring the area, looking for that blue house, and following the many train tracks that crisscrossed the old neighborhoods and industrial buildings.

The following morning Sterling spotted the house he had seen in his vision.

"Jack! Stop the car!" he shouted.

Pulling over to the curb, Jack eyed Sterling silently, unsure what to expect. Sterling stared intently at the dilapidated blue house, lips quivering. This place was where Charlotte's life had ended.

Frozen in place, Sterling scrutinized the suburban home, ignoring the children's playset in the backyard and the colorful flowers hanging from pots on the front porch. He noticed the 1959 Chevrolet stepside. At the back bumper, he saw the complete license plate number YAR537. This vehicle belonged to the murderer who kidnapped Charlotte. That was enough for Sterling who uncharacteristically threw the car door open, ready to pounce on the bastard.

He was stopped by pressure on his chest. Looking down, he stared at Jack's muscled arm holding him back.

"What are you doing, Jack?"

"No, the question is what are you doing?"

"Don't ask me how, Jack, but I know this is the place where Charlotte was murdered!"

"Murdered! All we have as legal evidence is that your girlfriend disappeared and nothing more. Now you're saying she was murdered? When did it come to that, kid? I don't have enough information to barge in and accuse these people of murder."

"Jack, trust me when I say this house is a murder scene."

"Even if that was true, I cannot let you burst in on this family and get this guy—not yet, not without a warrant. You must give me time to obtain a search warrant or else we lose to the son of a bitch because of a technicality."

"This fucker killed Charlotte, Jack. Do you want me to wait? Jack, I saw what he did with my own eyes!"

"Tell me, kid, even if I believe you, and I'm not saying I do, were you in there at the time of this so-called murder? What proof do you have that the murderer lives here? And how am I supposed to explain to another cop, a judge, and a jury how in hell you saw Charlotte's murder if you weren't there? If you weren't the one responsible? At best, you'd get locked in a looney bin, and I'd get kicked off the force. At worst—"

"Jack, please listen. I know where Charlotte's body is buried. Isn't that enough? Damn it, Jack, isn't that enough?"

"How on earth could you know that? Tell me!"

"I told you; I can't explain it any better. You have to trust me."

"All right, let's say you're right. Still, we cannot do anything without proof. I'm sorry, it's the way it is. Let's go back to the station and talk with my captain. We can tell him that you saw the suspect's truck fleeing the crime scene. That, in itself, should be enough for a search warrant."

"Sure, I suppose," Sterling responded while examining the house more closely. "Wait, Jack, something is wrong."

"What do you mean something is wrong?"

"It's not right is all. This particular house is not the house. Yes, it's old and blue, but this isn't the house. Damn it, Jack, this is not the house where the guy buried Charlotte, I'm certain!"

"Damn it, Sterling, you can't keep changing your mind!"

Unexpectedly, a bald man in his early thirties appeared out of the house, wearing sleeveless dark blue greasy coveralls. Even from a distance one could see his beard, thick and black, and the distinctive tattoos on his body. Carrying his lunch pail and coffee thermos, he jumped inside his truck. Slowly, he pulled out of his driveway and drove away. A minute later loud rumbling pipes echoed throughout the neighborhood as the engine came alive.

As the pickup passed them, the suspect stared straight ahead, never looking in the direction of the police cruiser as if he didn't have a care in the world. Then, the driver, calm and in no hurry, moved along. The pickup's loud mufflers echoed down the street and disappeared out of sight.

Sterling stared hatefully at the man as he saw the tattoo around the murderer's neck again. In addition, there was a skull with an open mouth. "That's him! Jack, I'm telling you that's the guy!"

"All right, Sterling, listen, I think this whole thing's a little wacko, but let's do this. Shit, who knows maybe—maybe we'll catch a break in the case,"

"Tell me, what do you propose?"

"First, we do some old-fashioned police work. Copying down the address. I have what I need for now—let's get out of here."

Leaving the house, Sterling felt as though he would die and could do nothing to ease his pain. Within those four walls lived a monster. Was the man a serial murderer or was it his first kill? For now there was no way of knowing. *But now that I've discovered this fiend, I won't let him escape justice.*

The long ride to the police station was a sad one. Try as Jack would, he could not help the deep hurt Sterling was experiencing. Thinking it best to get to the station as quickly as possible, he switched on his flashing lights. However, when their car approached a busy intersection and struggled to get through it, even with Jack repeatedly punching his blaring horn, Sterling remained stock-still and stared at the floor. For him, Charlotte was gone, and nothing would change that—no matter at what rate of speed the car traveled.

When they arrived at police headquarters, Jack stopped by his desk and removed his coat. His partner, Felix Solis, informed him that the lieutenant wanted to speak to him.

"Sure, thanks," Jack responded. "Sterling, come on. We need to see the captain."

When they appeared at the captain's office, Jack knocked and waited. Through the blinds he could see Lieutenant Jenkins talking with Captain Hartford. Hearing his name called, Jack walked inside with Sterling in tow.

"Captain, this young man beside me is named Sterling. He has something to say that I believe you will find interesting about the Charlotte Kemp case."

"Go on. Tell us what you know, young man," the captain responded.

"I believe I saw the truck and the suspect fleeing the scene the night Charlotte disappeared. I'm sure it was this guy, pretty sure."

"Mr. Sterling, can you describe the truck?"

"Yes, I sure can. It was a 1959 Chevrolet stepside pickup. It's the same type of truck my uncle drives."

"Can you tell us anything else, perhaps a license plate number?"

"Yes, I saw what looked like the number 37."

"Hmmm, all right, Danbury will take your statement. If

you have nothing else to add, please step out while Lieutenant Jenkins and I speak with Detective Danbury for a few minutes."

"Sure thing."

Captain Hartford had several books on civil law and municipal codes of the city before him. He looked up from the book and said, "Danbury, I've been searching through our city laws, and I can't find where it states that you, as an arresting officer, can place your suspect upside down inside a trash can—just can't find it anywhere."

"Hey, Cap, listen, yesterday when I was bringing the suspect into the station for questioning, the guy threatened to kick the shit out of me and rape my wife. The guy wouldn't shut his pie hole. When we arrived at the station, I'd had enough of his blubbering and decided to shut him up. Cap, look harder. I'm sure you'll find a civil code somewhere."

"Oh, ok, Danbury," the captain replied with resignation in his voice. Danbury had a habit of taking things a little further than he should. "Whatever you say, the Lieutenant and I just wanted to ensure it's in there. That will be all, Danbury,"

"You got it,"

When Danbury left the captain's office, he saw Sterling eagerly waiting at his desk.

"Well, what are we going to do now?"

"I'm hungry. Let's go get some breakfast,"

"What! You're hungry, Jack? What about Charlotte? Damn it, Jack, don't forget her murderer is still loose!"

"I have this covered, kid. Listen to me for a second. The D.A. doesn't get into his office until after nine o'clock if he doesn't have to appear in court this morning. Judge Harper not until ten o'clock. It's barely past eight now. We can do nothing directly; if we hope to see this through, it will be an all-day affair. Come on, let's go. I'm buying."

"Okay, I'm not hungry but okay if you insist."

As expected it took several hours before a search warrant could be obtained. In the meantime Danbury ran a background check on the suspect, Will Hanks, including his criminal history and financial records. Hanks had no prior arrests and seemed to be a model citizen.

Sterling's insistence that Will was the murderer drove the investigation onward. All that was required was to find Charlotte's body. For now Will was a suspect in a murder case and nothing more. Yes, he could be called into the station for questioning. But this soon, would it be wise? Danbury had his own way of doing things and wanted to gather as much intel as possible before Will was brought in and interrogated.

The standard procedure was to bring in the suspect and squeeze them to see if they would crack under stress. However, Jack believed Sterling and decided to skip the interview. Instead, his focus was on the house where Sterling said Charlotte's body was buried.

A break in the case came the following day when a rookie officer assigned to light duty because of a twisted ankle dropped off a copy of a tax bill for a property in the next county that Will Hanks had claimed on last year's taxes. The house once belonged to his mother, who left it to him in her will.

When Jack called and said he would be coming by to pick up Sterling, the excitement in Jack's voice suggested that a break in the case had finally come. Not asking where his friend was taking him, Sterling sat quietly and felt a strange enthusiasm building within him that increased with each passing mile. The pair drove to the blue-colored house and parked on the lonely street.

As he sat in the car, Sterling became overwhelmed by psychic activity. Unable to articulate his feelings, he knew his first love's remains were buried nearby in a solitary grave. He sat in the car, gathering the courage to approach.

Not comprehending Sterling's difficulty, Jack quickly got out of the car to look around. He stood on the sidewalk and eyed the property; he saw nothing out of the ordinary. Walking past a small, painted fence, Jack gawked around the backyard. The old house looked abandoned, with weeds growing everywhere and the mailbox stuffed with junk mail, giving the impression that its owner was gone.

Sterling finally gathered his courage, opened the car door, and stood next to Jack.

"What do you think, kid? Is this the place you saw in your vision?"

Sterling tried to deny his visions, despite what he'd told Jack the day before. He had explained that he "had feelings," but he'd never used the word "vision."

As he hesitated, not knowing what to say, Jack added. "Sterling, let's not play games with one another, all right? Listen to me for just a minute. I never told you this but the night of your parents' car crash, while I was trying to save your life, I could hear you talking to your mother."

"I don't remember, Jack. But okay, you heard me talking to my mother. What of it, Jack?"

"Your mother was dead! Yet, you conversed with her as if she were alive."

"I felt all alone, Jack, much like now." Feeling overwhelmed with emotion, Sterling broke out in tears and began sobbing.

"It will be all right, son. I know you've been through a lot. Tell me, is this where Charlotte Ann Kemp is buried?"

"Yes, Jack, she's right there," Sterling said, pointing to a small mound of freshly planted flowers.

"All right, you hang tight, kid. I'm calling for a search warrant and alerting the crime lab boys. They'll know what to do. For now let's return to the car and wait."

On a hunch Jack wrote his report and arrested Will

Hanks even before the crime investigators arrived. They searched for bodies and discovered not just Charlotte but four missing women who were all buried at Will's mother's home.

Jack tried his best to explain how the back door of his squad car accidentally opened and the suspect fell unconscious onto the roadway. He was taken to the emergency room with numerous broken bones, including a fractured jaw. Still, considering he was a cold-blooded murderer, even his defense attorney didn't pursue the matter.

He is still serving time on death row.

Sterling's thoughts returned to the present. By now Hanks was out of appeals and would fry for what he did to Charlotte and the other girls he murdered.

After the killer went to trial, Jack was promoted for his part in solving the case. Sterling got nothing but loneliness. He had lost Charlotte, his true love, and he wouldn't ever risk something happening to someone else he loved again; it was just too hard.

He lived a solitary life—he considered love an empty emotion he would never experience. It was never obtainable, just a foolish desire.

However, fate would prove him wrong.

Chapter 2
A Child's Haunting

It had been over seven years since Charlotte Kemp's murder. Now in his mid-twenties, Sterling found himself strolling alone on the grounds of a private estate. In the past several years, he had begun to gain a name for himself as a psychic detective, using his abilities to find missing children. Today he had been invited to the estate by a desperate mother, Lisa Howard, looking for her only son, Stewart.

Even at a young age, Sterling had already developed rigorous standards to help him choose which of the many cases that came to his attention he would pursue. It was difficult to withstand the tear-filled pleas of the many parents who called on him, but it was worth it. He only had so much time—and so much energy. These cases were always exhausting. He had learned to tell which parents he could help from who would never know what happened to their child.

Lisa Howard had passed Sterling's rigorous standards and proved that she would do anything to find her son. Now he was strolling on the private grounds of her forty-acre estate near Portsmouth, New Hampshire, considering his next steps. He admired the lush landscape decorated with pine, maple, and ash and the beautiful flowerbeds clustered near the home, a stately mansion in the middle of the property.

Made of stone, it stood cold and uncaring. It had been built over a hundred years ago by the Howard family, whose name had become synonymous with wealthy aristocrats.

Looking at the green surroundings, one could see the rolling hills off in the distance. The estate was completely private, with a stone wall surrounding the entire perimeter, protecting it from unwelcomed guests. As Sterling continued his walk, he came upon a pond. There, jetting halfway into the water, was a small dock. As he walked upon the creaky timbers, he noticed threatening clouds brewing overhead, driven by a cold wind that blew across his back. Lifting his coat collar around his neck, he stared across the dark water, thinking about little Stewart, the missing boy. An alarming disturbance began deep in his soul. Something ominous had happened here in this peaceful place; he could feel the disruption it left behind.

At the end of the pier, two stone lions stared across the water as if guarding some old family secrets. Unable to speak, possibly they alone were witnesses to some event that took place here that was so horrible that no one could conceive of it.

Ronald Howard, the wealthy lone survivor of the Howard name, had developed mumps as a child and became sterile. Unable to provide the family with a suitable heir, Ronald thought when he met a young waitress at the country club, an attractive single mother with one child, her son could naturally fill the role of the family's successor. He could be molded into the family likeness and carry on the Howard name. Although his upper-crust society pals warned Ronald not to marry a lower-class woman, he ignored their pleas and wedded Lisa anyway.

And Lisa Grubb`s only child Stewart became Ronald's sole heir.

However, things did not go smoothly for the new family—and only worsened over time. Eight-year-old Stewart was not interested in the family business and showed little interest in finance and the stock market. He wanted to be a little boy—not an heir to a fortune. He wanted to play cowboys and Indians with the Howard servants. That was much more interesting than learning about corporate takeovers and mergers.

By age ten, Stewart could barely remember the time before his mother married—a time when he had been happy. His mother's attention was replaced with toys and games as Lisa felt torn between her son and her new husband, who demanded all her attention.

The social events for the rich left little time for what a child needed in his life. And Stewart became a bored, unhappy child who spent long, tedious days with tutors and servants while his mother was hardly ever seen. Stewart's father taught him the same way. He thought it was the only way to help his adopted son learn the valuable lessons of the corporate world. And when nothing else seemed to work, the rod of understanding was used without restraint.

Sterling had asked to sleep in Stewart's room, where he could be surrounded by the boy's physical belongings and connect with his spiritual essence, and had been there a few days. There he would learn of the child's hardships and disappointments—and the use of Ronald's garden hose for Stewart`s correction.

Yes, Stewart Howard had gone missing at the mall. The police report claimed a thin man had been seen grabbing Stewart there. An all-points bulletin was issued for the man and child.

But Sterling felt an energy disturbance around the small

pier as if a path had been created. That path was plainly legible for those with the gift to follow. He felt in his soul that this place was where Stewart had died. Although Lisa said she still hoped for the boy's safe return, Sterling was sure that was a complete waste of time.

As Sterling closed his eyes, concentrating on his surroundings, he heard a man's voice.

"Are you speaking to the fishes now, Sterling?"

He turned around and saw Ronald's attaché, Justin, behind him.

A bald man with a muscular build wore a dark suit with a bow tie wrapped around his massive neck. He looked like a butler but was much more than that. And he and Sterling disliked each other at first sight.

Sterling, however, had long become accustomed to hiding his feelings. "Yes," he replied and turned to continue his contemplation of the tranquil pond. "The quiet here allows me time to think and clear my mind,"

Justin offensively remarked, "I didn't know you had a thing for dead fishes, Sterling. But then again, I thought you were a weirdo as soon as I met you."

Sterling ignored his comment, stepped toward the pier's edge, and looked down into the murky water.

"Mr. Howard is growing tired of your constant snooping around. He suggests you give up your search for the brat. He's gone, and that's all there is to it."

Turning back around, Sterling stared at the man and said, "I'm not so sure."

Justin laughed. "Sterling, go find a crystal ball and search the mall where the kid went missing. No doubt you'll find him there playing his favorite arcade games."

Sterling, undaunted by the big goon's remark, said, "Mrs. Lisa Howard hired me; I'm not leaving until Stewart is found—go tell that to your boss!"

"Yeah, well, this much I do know. You won't find

Stewart inspecting fishes in the pond!"

An awkward pause fell between the two men.

"Go tell your boss that we are having a spiritual gathering in Stewart's room this evening—around ten. It will help us unlock the secrets to where Stewart is being imprisoned."

Again, silence fell as Justin stared at Sterling. Finally, he turned away and said, "I'll inform Mr. Howard. Once you are done with this farce, I'm sure we'll be rid of you once and for all."

"Yes," Sterling replied. "The feeling is mutual."

"Is that all you have to tell me?"

"I have nothing else but to say that nothing makes sense."

"Nothing makes sense? What's that supposed to mean?" Justin asked, with a puzzled look on his face.

Sterling gazed out at the pond without explaining.

Justin shook his head and walked away. The man could never understand that for someone with Sterling's abilities the trail the deceased left behind was readable in ways that would not make any sense to the unbelieving.

Looking at the edge of the tiny dock's pilings that trailed down into the water, Sterling could see the signs that someone's life ended there. Perhaps a family suicide? But whatever it was, a very slight presence disrupted the flow of energy around this pond that was distinctive in many ways.

This energy is unique for every individual that exists on the earth. It is as though someone has taken a photograph in time of the surrounding area, and in the midst of the photo is a life force. Yes, a precious life made a difference, whether good or bad. We don't just exist on this planet; no, we leave an aura of our existence behind after our passing.

This aura was how Sterling was able to know when someone died, their trace that they had left behind. Perhaps a trail of horror when the individual knew that they were to die or found themselves struggling to stay alive. Then, when their spirit left their earthly body, they surrendered their life at that precise moment. It left behind a break in the balance between the living and the dead—the sharp broken line in time and space.

As Sterling closed his eyes, he saw this break in the fabric of life. Finding himself completely alone, he left his current surroundings and began to envision the sounds of Stewart screaming for help, imagining such an event, playing it out. He fine-tuned his senses to the echoes that surrounded him.

Trying his best to ignore the sounds coming from the nearby waterfowl, Sterling began to hear a child crying; the words seemed muffled as if traveling from a great distance away. He let his consciousness drift. He closed off all influences from the outside world. His breathing slowed; his heart rate slowed. He listened to the steady beating becoming slower and slower within his chest.

While his life ran from his body, he stood frozen in time and space. Focused, he concentrated on the muffled screams coming from far away. Sterling tried to follow their origin, seemingly leading him to the pond beside him. The closer he got to the cries, the colder and darker everything around him became. Somewhere not far away the child was calling out for help. Spiritually speaking, he moved his thoughts toward the unknown as the light around him faded, causing him to wonder where he was traveling.

More clearly than before, he heard the child's cries and felt himself drawn into the icy depths of an unnamed tomb. As he got closer to the source, the words spoken started to make more sense.

Although his mind and soul couldn't understand what was being said, Sterling recognized the voice as Stewart, calling from a deep chasm in his heart.

"Mommy, help me."

The unambiguous emotions of the young child's cries affected Sterling in the most profound way possible. It wasn't the least gratifying to hear Stewart's call for help. Sterling felt a spiritual connection to the boy's sadness, which wounded his soul. Tears ran down his face as he understood the hopeless feeling of the innocent child fighting to find his way home.

Here was where the answers lay; here was the place where something horrible happened. Sterling, struggling to come closer, noticed his focus was distracted by a distant roaring sound. Flashes of light erupted around him, forcing him back to reality.

The cries for help abruptly ended. Sterling opened his eyes to the world around him—and saw no one. The only signs of life came from the squawking birds overhead. Standing alone, he saw the clouds overhead pushed about by a passing breeze and the waves from the pond slapping the shoreline. Yet, all around him, he was alone, and if he hadn't known better, he would have thought the cries from the great beyond had been nothing more than his imagination playing tricks on him.

While he stood there a brightly colored cardinal flew overhead and landed on one of the pier's pilings. Suddenly, it began chirping as if it had something important to tell Sterling. But he didn't speak fowl so admired its beauty. However, the bird's presence seemed peculiar in many ways. Having studied different cultures throughout the world, Sterling considered the red cardinal's arrival to be synonymous with the death of a loved one.

Sterling stood admiring it until the bird dropped to the ground, excitedly making quick little nervous gestures as it looked about. It chirped impatiently.

Something unknown and hidden was there. As Sterling curiously watched, the bird danced around the wooden planks of the dock, flapped its elegant wings, and flew away as quickly as it had arrived, leaving Sterling to ponder the reason for its visit.

After Stewart's disappearance, the police searched everywhere but had no clue where he had disappeared. After probing the entire mall, which turned up empty, they searched the estate and every room throughout the house but found nothing. According to Lisa, they also explored the estate's property, including the pond, but still found no trace of the boy's body.

Lisa's husband, Ronald, had no objections to unearthing the ground around the pond. He told the police that he wanted to remodel that area anyway. The heavy equipment was ordered after the crime investigators left; it arrived the next day and completed the repairs quickly. Everything around the pond looked new and pristine.

Sterling felt alone and saddened by what he had just experienced. Walking back to the house, he was distracted from his thoughts when he saw a rider galloping toward him on a chestnut stallion. It was Lisa Howard. Although she was still a ways off, Sterling remembered Lisa saying that yellow roses were her favorite. Walking over to the nearby rose garden that decorated the stone walkway, he plucked a yellow rose from one of the bushes.

As she rode up he bowed to her admiringly, as if she were a queen of noble birth, and said, "Good afternoon, Mrs. Howard. How was your ride?"

The beautiful animal approached slowly; the large stallion stopped a foot from Sterling, breathing hard after its gallop and blowing out spit between its bridle and teeth. As Lisa pulled tightly on the reins, the animal raised its head upward in submission.

"It's such a lovely day. I couldn't resist taking Trigger for a stroll. It was our favorite pastime, both Stewart and me," Lisa said warmly.

Petting her horse, Sterling watched as Lisa dismounted.

"So, tell me, how was your afternoon? We missed you at breakfast. Were you not feeling well, Sterling?"

"No, it wasn't that. Truthfully, I'm getting the feeling that your husband, Ronald, is growing tired of my presence and is anxious for me to leave."

"No, you cannot leave yet. You haven't found Stewart," Lisa cried out desperately. "The police have not found the kidnappers. Ronald believes that more than one person is involved in Stewart's abduction!"

"Yes, that's a reasonable conclusion," Sterling responded. Knowing the desperation the young mother felt, he wasn't going to dash her hopes of finding her son alive, but the truth was that both he and the murderer knew that the boy was dead.

Despondent, Lisa gazed out across the pond. Seeing her sadness, Sterling handed her the rose he had plucked earlier. She looked at its petite, fragile beauty and smiled.

"You always seem to know how to make me smile, Sterling."

"It's a gift."

"Perhaps I should have never told you that yellow was my favorite color. Possibly, with your physic powers of observation, you would have already guessed that, though?"

"Yes, it's possible. Who can say?" he said laughingly.

Lisa laughed with him, then quickly looked grave.

"Promise me, Sterling, that you won't give up searching for Stewart. Not until we can catch the monsters that took him. Make me this promise," she cried desperately. "I have no one else willing to listen to me."

Sterling took her in his arms, holding her carefully, comfortingly. He was touched by her love for her son and could not bear to dash her hopes. Stewart would never return to the mother who loved him but could he tell Lisa the truth? No, not yet! Instead, he looked at the desperate woman and said, "I will stay, to the dislike of your husband, and together we will find your son."

"Thank you," Lisa said tearfully.

She broke away from his arms and mounted her horse, gripping the reins tightly. Turning away briefly to hide her watery eyes, she asked, "We will see you at dinner this evening?"

"Yes, of course, at seven then?"

"Goodbye, for now, Sterling—and thank you."

Turning the large animal, she kicked the horse and galloped away, leaving him alone.

The stroll back to the mansion allowed Sterling time to think. How would Lisa take the news of her son's demise? How would it affect this Shangri-La world of hers? He hoped Lisa was resilient enough to recover from her son's death and that in time she'd get over this harrowing experience and not be scarred for life. Only time would tell. An adage came to mind: A time to mourn and a time to heal.

Arriving at the estate, Sterling walked past the massive ornate doors leading to the grand entrance. Inside expensive Spanish mosaic tile decorated the foyer in a circular pattern—antique furniture decorated the room. Down two hallways leading to other parts of the house lay plush and brightly colored Persian carpets. Tall stained-glass windows allowed enough light into the room to seem pleasant but not intrusive.

Sterling wished for nothing more than to rest before dinner and trudged up the spiral staircase to the third floor toward his room. Arriving on the third floor, he began the long walk to Stewart's bedroom at the back of the house.

He had only walked a short way when Justin, Ronald's goon, came out of Stewart's bedroom. He smiled insincerely.

"Excuse me, psychic man,"

Sterling was angry. This goon had been snooping inside Stewart's bedroom—where his suitcase was stored. He wanted to tell the guy to get lost but thought better of it. Instead, he responded politely.

"Yes, what is it, Justin?"

"There is someone who wishes to speak to you. The man is waiting in the library."

"Who is it?"

"It's Mr. Howard's attorney. He wants to speak with you if you have a moment."

"Yes, of course. Justin, let me ask you a question. Why were you snooping around in Stewart's bedroom?"

"No, you have it all wrong. I wasn't snooping around. I was simply searching for you."

Ignoring Justin's blatant lie, Sterling said, "Tell the lawyer I'll be down shortly."

"Of course," the lapdog answered, then walked away.

After refreshing himself, Sterling arrived at the library a short time later. Walking into the room, he saw the family lawyer drinking a Scotch. Standing to his feet, the man in the dark suit approached.

"You must be Sterling?"

"Yes, I understand you wanted to see me. Tell me, how can I help you?"

"My name is Barkley, from the Barkley and Sandler law firm." The lawyer reached out to shake Sterling's hand.

Sterling, whose dealings with lawyers weren't always pleasant, ignored the lawyer's salutation and sat down across from him on the sofa. Sterling had testified in many criminal cases, and each experience had left a sour taste in his mouth. Since Charlotte's murder Sterling had advocated for children's rights. But more often than not it was too late when he was asked to help.

"Tell me, Mr. Barkley, what can I do for you?"

"My firm represents the Howard family in all legal matters. I'm here today to protect my clients. We cannot allow their name to be misrepresented or appear in the tabloids."

"Yes, and what does that have to do with me?"

"Simply put, your involvement in the search for the missing boy named Stewart Howard—"

"What involvement would that be, sir?"

Barkley took another sip of the expensive Scotch and proclaimed, "Mr. Howard is quite concerned that you're snooping around and could turn up some skeletons in the Howard family closet. As legal counsel I must inform you that such a thing would make you liable if said information found its way to the newspapers."

Sterling sat back and thought for a moment before responding carefully. "Can I ask you a question, Mr. Barkley?"

"Yes, of course."

"What do you feel is more important, finding a lost child who has been taken from his mother or the name of some decrepit aristocratic family?"

Barkley slowly took another sip of his drink and attempted to intimidate Sterling by looking down his nose at him. Sterling chuckled to himself. He had faced his worst monsters and demons—a lawyer couldn't scare him. Finally, the lawyer responded.

"I had little faith that you would understand the importance of what I have said. Your caring mother has been fortunate enough to marry above her class. Mr. Howard, out of the kindness of his heart, took both Lisa and her little imp as his own. He gave them the chance to raise themselves above their miserable status in life and become something great."

"Is this what you and Mr. Howard believe? Out of Ronald's kindness, he has given Stewart and his mother a chance to upgrade themselves, as you call it. Sadly, since little Stewart has gone missing, his mother and I fear something horrible has occurred. But you refer to him as nothing but a little imp?" Sterling's hand retracted into a fist as he held it tightly against his leg as if willing himself not to take a swing at the lawyer.

"Apparently, you do not see the bigger picture here, young man!"

"No, you're wrong; I see perfectly. Probably a good thing. But listen, I have grown tired and wish to rest before dinner so if you would please excuse me, Mr. Barkley—"

Leaving the library, Sterling saw Justin standing by as if ready to intervene. As Sterling walked past him, neither man spoke.

Sterling returned to his room—he knew in his heart that the answer to Stewart's disappearance would soon be revealed. Then Lisa would know where her son's remains were buried, and she would have closure. Not the hoped-for reunion with her son but at least she would no longer search for her missing boy or wait for that dreaded phone call from the police saying they had discovered his body.

Arriving at Stewart's bedroom door, he opened it to find Lisa sitting on the tiny bed, holding a picture of her missing son. Tears ran down her cheeks.

"Oh, excuse me, Mrs. Howard, I didn't know you were in the room."

"Sterling, please come inside." Scooting over to make room, she cried, "I wish I knew who has taken my son. Do you have any news about Stewart's whereabouts? Anything would be greatly appreciated. Please, Sterling, I'm so desperate to learn the truth."

"Mrs. Howard—Lisa—I'm trying to connect with Stewart's aura. I find it difficult because he wasn't a strong or vibrant soul. How do I say this without sounding harsh or cruel? Stewart wasn't a strong influence in the world we occupy. Like many young boys, his interest was rudimentary; having fun mattered most to him and perhaps his next meal. That's to be expected.

"And by the way, please do me a small favor. My name is not Mr. Sterling; it's simply Sterling. I would prefer that."

"Yes, of course, Sterling, it is—um—Sterling, I want to ask you, please tell me, what is it that you see when you enter the spiritual world searching for someone lost?"

"In that place I have experienced things that would terrify most living beings. I'm never alone in the spiritual world—especially when someone has suffered mistreatment or death. I admit that I have become fearful of seeing ghostly images and murders. They appear to me begging, not with words that one can hear but just as powerful motions. They search for understanding of what has happened to them and wait for justice."

"That's very sad."

"The perpetrators responsible for taking little Stewart believe that their wicked deeds will go unpunished, and they go about their lives feeling that the wrong they've done won't ever be noticed. They feed and kill without fear of any consequence, no matter the cost they inflict to innocent lives with their twisted desires."

"Sterling—I'm nobody's fool! I'm not sure if you realize this, but you mentioned the word 'kill.'"

Sterling paused. "I have to use that word simply because of the unknown."

Lisa again began to cry. Turning to Sterling, tears in her eyes, she said, "I do not believe that Stewart is alive. I don't know why I feel this way, but it haunts me in ways I can't explain. I haven't said anything to Ronald because he's hopeful that we will find Stewart alive; he loves that child so much and has done nothing but weep for him since his disappearance."

"I understand. I want to have a gathering of sorts after dinner."

"What do you mean, Sterling?"

"It's something I have done in the past with other

families. It's a way to connect with those who have been taken from them. We meet in the missing person's place of comfort. Everyone involved in Stewart's life must attend this meeting for no reason other than to fill in the gaps. Where the victim feels the most secure in life, we will find the answers we seek. In that place we search for what happened to Stewart."

"I cannot say with certainty that Ronald will join us."

"Why not?"

"You must understand how difficult this has been on Ronald. Whenever I suggest that we talk about what has happened to our son, he breaks down and cries. This reaction is from a man who has always been the provider for the family. He feels responsible for not protecting our son."

"Ronald was at the mall at the time of Stewart's disappearance, wasn't he?"

"Yes, unfortunately. Well, it's getting late, and I must prepare myself for dinner." Standing to leave, Lisa paused and asked, "See you downstairs, Sterling?"

"Yes, of course," he answered and watched her leave.

Now alone Sterling felt tired and closed his eyes; he allowed his mind to drift. Unexpectedly, he remembered Charlotte. The memory of her smile soothed him. He felt his body jerk as his muscles began to relax and wind down as he drifted. He had no particular visions or thoughts. He was content to lie there and dream of happier times; they felt like dreams rather than memories of long ago. This solitary life he lived—no wonder he was always alone.

Frustrated, he felt weighed down by this wretched gift of being a mediator between the living and the dead. The simple task of falling asleep was often a losing proposition. He opened his eyes and stared at the shadows on the walls, watching them move. Slowly, the colors in the room faded to a soothing gray. He began to revisit a favorite imaginary place, a place he had never been, but the thought of it made him happy.

Closing his eyes, he found himself sailing a yacht. He felt that being aboard the small vessel would take him far away from his troubles and sadness with no particular destination in mind. Looking ahead, he navigated through the deep crystal blue waters of the Caribbean.

Sterling imagined the warm sun overhead and dreamed of being nude. Here, upon the open waters, he could relax and let go of all the horrid dreams and visions that haunted his every waking hour. What mattered most was the solace and peaceful rest this imaginary place provided.

Somehow, upon the sailing craft of his dreams, he felt protected; he watched the wind fill his sails, pushing him along. The night sky appeared above him. A vast array of stars twinkled brightly.

This dream was so pleasant that he never wanted to wake. Everything felt right. He smiled. His unhappiness faded, and he breathed a sigh of relief, allowing himself to relax further into his dream state.

Without warning an uninvited flash of numbers burst into his dream. The time—2:12 a.m.—appeared brightly in red. Not knowing what it meant, he awoke in a flash. Sitting up in a panic, he wondered, what reason was there be for seeing that time? What could it mean?

Sterling turned to look at the clock on the nightstand; the time displayed was 6:35 p.m. in bold red numbers. *That's strange; it's the same clock from my vision.* Picking it up, he stared at it briefly; it seemed to be just an alarm clock and nothing more. It must not be the clock that held significance, but the numbers and how they related to him. Setting down the clock, he promised to give it some more thought later. But for now he needed to get ready for dinner. He quickly showered and dressed.

Sometime later, appearing in the drawing-room, Sterling saw Ronald, deep in thought, with a cocktail in his hand. The overweight, wrinkle-faced master of the house looked up briefly.

"Good evening, Mr. Sterling."

It is not worth explaining that it isn't his actual name; it is simply not worth the argument. Sterling sat in one of the high-back chairs and eyed his host, wondering what held his attention so intently.

"Mr. Sterling, would you care for a drink?"

"Yes, I wouldn't mind."

"Name your poison."

"A Bourbon Rickey. Bourbon, some sparkling water, with a twist of lime, please."

Turning to the nearby butler, Ronald nodded, then speedily a drink appeared. Tasting the bourbon, Sterling could tell it was both old and expensive.

"I'm glad I caught you alone, Mr. Sterling. I have talked to my wife, and she and I have discussed your desire to meet with the two of us in Stewart's room after dinner. Lisa explained to me that you wish to perform some séance of sorts. My opinion is that it's a complete waste of time."

Sterling stared back into Ronald's bloodshot eyes. "That's disappointing to hear you say that, Ronald."

"Yes, that is the way it is, I'm afraid. Furthermore, I feel that your visit here needs to end. You're scaring the servants and making them nervous."

"Ronald, let me ask you something. Is it possible that you're the one who is nervous and uncomfortable, not the servants? Perhaps you'll be more comfortable if I give up searching for your stepson?"

Sterling took another sip of Bourbon Rickey; it went down as smoothly as his latest rebuttal.

Ronald laughed nervously.

"Look, Ronald, I realize you don't like me or my methods. But I assure you that I have nothing but the best intentions regarding finding Stewart. I feel he wants to be found. But I have to ask: Why are there no demands for ransom? Could it be that the supposed kidnappers are not interested in money but maybe the power it gives them to see you suffer?"

"Oh, I'm sure a ransom note is coming soon."

"Ronald, you should know it's not just the spiritual world I investigate. I have also looked into the Howard name. You've been involved in hostile takeovers and mergers. Frankly, I have heard that your family hasn't always treated people fairly. It's been reported in the newspapers that you are nothing more than a crook in an expensive suit."

"Watch your mouth, Sterling," Ronald demanded.

"Or what? Mr. Howard, tell me!" Sterling accepted the challenge before him and stared back at the patriarch of the Howard family, ready for any confrontation.

Just then Lisa stepped into the drawing room. Sterling looked over at her, noticing Ronald's wan face. He stood as she entered the room, seeing, too, that her husband didn't bother with this small courtesy. Sterling noticed Justin in the shadows out of the corner of his eye. He looked ready to strike if called upon to defend his master.

Ronald's frown quickly disappeared. He lifted his glass. "Good evening, dear, won't you join us?"

Lisa, appearing in evening wear, turned to her husband and said, "Darling, be a dear, and get me my favorite drink?"

She sounded as if she were trying to pretend this was just another typical night—when everyone in the room knew it was anything but a typical night at the Howards.

"Yes, of course," Ronald answered.

He again nodded at the butler, and a moment later a sherry hurriedly arrived.

Sterling, raised by his uncle, had been taught proper manners. He remained standing until she sat on the sofa, then he sat down again. Looking back at Ronald, Sterling mentioned his disappointment at hearing that Ronald would not be joining them for the gathering that evening.

Lisa turned to her husband. "Darling, you're not joining us this evening for the gathering in Stewart's room?"

"Unfortunately, I have a pressing engagement at our corporate office in Shanghai that requires my utmost expertise. I'm leaving within the hour for the airport. I will return in a few days."

"This is news to me." Lisa sounded disappointed.

"Darling, have you told Mr. Sterling the good news?" Ronald asked brashly.

"What news, my love?"

"The news about our search to find a suitable match to carry on the proud name of Howard. You might find this interesting, Mr. Sterling, especially since my lovely wife cannot get impregnated by me and cannot give me a suitable heir. I have diligently searched historical birth records and discovered that my father had a bastard son living in Europe. For a small price the man agreed to provide his seed to artificially inseminate my wife, thereby persevering the name of Howard for generations to come," Ronald said smugly.

"Darling, I thought we would discuss this further in private. I have never agreed to anything yet because Stewart is still missing. I told you it wasn't the right time to discuss having another child. Not until we have found Stewart. You know this." Lisa, upset, finished her sherry in one swallow.

Angered by his wife's announcement, the gloating autocratic asshole finished his cocktail, slamming down the glass upon the table. He turned and nodded his head at Justin. The silent gesture meant it was time to depart. Ronald placed a small kiss on his wife's cheek and left.

With Ronald gone, the mood was light and cordial during dinner sometime later. Afterward, Lisa asked Sterling to come to the library for some brandy. Throughout the rest of the evening Lisa looked anxious and stared at her watch.

Suddenly, she looked up and announced, "I'm ready to begin this séance. Just tell me when you're ready!"

"Lisa, listen to me for a moment," Sterling responded. "If you would rather we could make it another time; I completely understand. We don't have to do this now. Perhaps it would be better if we didn't have a gathering, simply because of the way you're feeling,"

"Why did he have to say that?" she said, referring to her husband's earlier tirade. "Why did he bring up carrying on the Howard name? I don't understand it."

"Lisa, listen to me. I want to help you find Stewart, but you have to free yourself of this anger toward Ronald right now. You have to free your emotions and your mind and your spirit as well. All of these have to come together. Then, only then, can we search for the answers that we need."

Lisa paused, crossing her arms and narrowing her eyes. She looked back at Sterling.

"I'm ready to do this, damn it! Let's find Stewart. When can we begin?"

OVER THE NEXT FEW DAYS, each morning would bring the same appeal over breakfast, "Sterling, how soon are we going to have a séance?"

After several days of Sterling putting off the séance, one morning, shortly past breakfast, Sterling announced, "Tonight there will be a full moon, making it the perfect time to have a séance. We can begin at midnight."

"Where should we have this séance?"

"We need a place that's quiet and comfortable. I have more success when both the seeker and I are in a comfortable position, allowing one's body to relax and releasing one's soul from the confines of this world."

"Okay," Lisa said agreeably, "How about we use Stewart's bedroom as you suggested?"

"Fine, that will work."

"I can't wait. I feel in my heart that something will be revealed. I'm not sure what it will be and, truthfully, I'm not sure I'm ready to learn what happened to my little boy. Sterling, I must know the truth."

"I completely understand, Lisa. Let's meet in Stewart's bedroom at midnight."

"Do you need anything? I mean to perform the séance?"

"Yes, please arrange for your servants to bring me as many candles as possible, including matches, of course. Inside Stewart's bedroom we will travel on a spiritual journey to places unknown. Everything has to be perfect."

"I promise you'll have everything you need."

"I'll see you tonight. I must prepare myself."

"Tonight I'll finally have my answer," Lisa announced.

Sterling kept to himself throughout the day, meditating and clearing his mind. He refused to eat and only sipped water. Late in the afternoon there was a knock on the door. Sterling answered it and found a servant holding a bag of candles.

Sterling thanked the man and arranged the candles throughout the room by taking the bag from the servant's hand. Shortly before midnight Lisa arrived. She found all the candles lit, giving a warm glow to the room.

"Tell me, what should I do?" Lisa asked.

"Lie down upon Stewart's bed and get comfortable. I need you to close your eyes to all outside influences."

Sitting on the floor next to the edge of the bed, Sterling said, "Lisa, let me hold your hand."

"Okay—certainly." She placed her hand in his, took a long breath, then exhaled.

Crossing his legs, Sterling cleared his mind and said, "I want you to imagine Stewart playing—perhaps a distant memory when you remember the two of you being happy and not afraid."

"Are you going to read my mind, Sterling?" Lisa remarked with a chuckle.

"If only I could. But no, I cannot read your mind, Lisa. What I can do is follow your motherly connection to your son. Let me explain what I mean. A spiritual connection between the two lives transpires when a mother carries a child for nine months in her womb. This phenomenon cannot be broken or destroyed. The most powerful force known to man is and always will be a mother's love for her child. That's why I want you to take me to that joyful time when you and Stewart were happiest."

"I understand."

"However, I must warn you that while you remember that event and another thought pops into your head, then the spiritual connection will be broken, and we will have to try connecting to the spiritual world another time."

"Okay, I've got it," Lisa agreed, "Now I'm ready. Let's get started."

"I need you to close your eyes and describe the events of that particular day in detail. I will follow you through your consciousness. I cannot control where your thoughts will take us; you're driving the bus, so to speak. I'm just an observer."

"Yes, again, I understand. Let's get started on our journey to the unknown."

"Good, now close your eyes and tell me about your favorite memories of Stewart."

"Stewart was just six years old, and Ronald had taken us to the park. We were only dating then, and it was such a beautiful day. There was a traveling circus in town, and Ronald thought it would be nice to take Stewart to a circus. That day Ronald picked us up in a limousine. We were both so thrilled to be traveling in such style, and it was something that we hadn't ever experienced. Although I worked two jobs to support us, we could never afford to take a day off work to visit the circus; money was tight."

Lisa continued her recollections. As they entered the festival, the crowds around them closed in tightly. Sterling could see the happy couple walking about the circus by connecting with her memory. He saw Stewart holding Ronald and his mother's hand, looking pleased. Ronald felt romantic and pulled Lisa close and began kissing her—and she let go of her grip upon Stewart. Before they knew it the boy was lost in the crowd.

Suddenly, remembering the event, Sterling felt Lisa's grip tighten. Distress filled her as she began to describe what happened next.

Sterling could see the events unfold, coming to life as if they were played out on a big screen. In a panic Lisa turned to Ronald, shouting, "Where's Stewart?"

The man looked around and said, "Don't worry, my dear, he cannot have gotten far."

They both called out Stewart's name but their voices did not travel far in the crowded, noisy midway.

Suddenly thrust into this place and time, Sterling felt every ounce of terror that Lisa had experienced. And through her emotion of fear, he followed Stewart into the crowd of circus attendees. The bond that Lisa had with her son was Sterling's compass. As he followed it like a bloodhound, he caught the spiritual scent of something invisible yet natural and powerful—again, the bond between child and mother.

What he saw was Stewart near a body of water. Now he completely ignores Lisa as she explains how she and Ronald searched for Stewart at the circus. Sterling is focused intently on Stewart. Traveling to a place of darkness, he hears muffled cries for help.

Drawing closer to the source, Sterling finds himself in a dark pond with large boulders at the sandy bottom. The water is murky and hard to see through. Reaching the bottom, Sterling sees a blackness that allows little light to penetrate. He can hear Stewart calling much more clearly than before.

To his horror, he feels something touching him. Turning around, he sees a young child reaching out with bony little fingers. His eyes are dark—without life. His boyish blond hair floats just above his head, and his face is the color blue. He shows no sign of life until suddenly, opening his eyes wide, the boy screams.

"Mommy."

This vision was so disturbing that Sterling wanted to end it and escape but he couldn't. He had to help Lisa. So despite his horror—for Lisa, for this poor child crying for his mommy as he was caught in a loop reliving his ghastly death—Sterling focused on Stewart. He could hear Lisa reliving the events of that day in the background, completely unaware of where her son was or that he was dead. Sterling remained steadfast in a trance.

Stewart closed his eyes again as if sleeping, a silent prisoner in that cold, dark place he couldn't escape. Sterling noticed something else: a thick chain wrapped around the boy's body. Whoever had placed him in this dark, watery cave didn't want his remains to float to the surface.

As Sterling concentrated on Stewart's surroundings, he saw a sandy bottom with three distinct, large boulders. Looking over at the slimy walls of the cave, he saw an unusually bright-colored fish swimming nearby, then another—a total of four fish, all the same species: redear sunfish. Sterling looked up and saw the pilings of a small pier near the boy's body. As he concentrated on the surroundings where Stewart was held prisoner, he heard another voice.

"Mom, Mom."

It wasn't Stewart. This time a girl's voice cried out, weak and distressed.

He tried to locate the voice—and his vision changed. He

saw a flock of crows building a nest in towering trees. What did this new image mean? One particular crow flew down from its perch, landing beneath telephone lines in a small, rocky clearing. It pecked at a shiny object on the ground, picked up the item, and flew back into the tall trees, placing the thing in its nest.

Sterling examined the area, thinking it odd and sinister. Was this a place he was meant to visit in his future? Abruptly, Lisa's voice became louder and more evident. He was losing the portal to the spiritual world. He opened his eyes to a surprised Lisa staring back at him. She quickly set up in the bed.

"Well, what did you see?"

Sterling stood and began walking about the room. He considered his words carefully. But before he had time to say anything, Lisa put her hands to her face.

"Stewart is dead, isn't he?" She began to cry. "I should never have agreed to let Ronald take Stewart to the mall. If he hadn't, Stewart would still be alive today. But my mother was in the hospital. I wanted to be with her. When Ronald told me something dreadful had happened and to get home immediately, I rushed back as soon as possible, only to discover that some sick monsters had taken Stewart."

Sterling walked over to Lisa and laid his hand on her shoulder.

"Yes, I believe that your son, Stewart, is gone—I'm so sorry, Lisa. I wish I could have better news for you but, unfortunately, I do not."

With desperation in her eyes, she sobbed, "Can you at least tell me where he is?"

"No, I cannot tell you exactly where his body is located. But I believe he will be found soon."

Lisa stood up. "Sterling, you have fulfilled your bargain. You told me what I wanted to know; that's why I hired you so I guess you can leave anytime. But please, I need you to find his body."

Sterling reached over and held her close as she burst into tears. He didn't want to leave her with the weight of her son's death crashing down upon her. He tried to hold and comfort her, but it wasn't his place. Her son was gone.

Pushing herself away from Sterling's embrace, she looked at him.

"Sterling, thank you for your kindness. Please tell me you'll find my son's body for me before you leave."

"This experience involving Stewart is troubling. You have my word. I will find your son if it's humanly possible. Stewart is nearby. He's here, somewhere on this property, and I cannot make the connection between him and me. I can't leave until I find him—I will not leave, no matter what!"

There was nothing left to say. An awkward silence fell as they looked into each other's eyes for the longest time. Sterling wondered what might have happened between them if they had met under different circumstances. Then Lisa turned and walked away, leaving Sterling to feel miserable knowing that her son's body was lost and no one knew where—that is, except the murderer.

A short time later Sterling walked outside for some fresh air and shook off the sadness he felt for little Stewart. The night sky looked bright, filled with twinkling stars above. As he walked the estate grounds to clear his head, he wondered about the significance of the single crow taking the shiny object and hiding it in its nest—perhaps soon another journey to the unknown.

A thought came to Sterling's mind. How much more do I have to give of myself to those who need my cursed gift? As Sterling looked up at Lisa's bedroom window, a light appeared. Turning away, he whispered, "Oh Lisa, sweet, innocent Lisa. The only thing I can do for you is to find your little boy's body and return him to you!"

The day after the séance Sterling felt troubled. He was close to discovering where Stewart's body was kept. After dinner he went on a walk. Following the stone pathway leading to the small pond, he saw a tiny light illuminating the dock and reflecting on the water's surface, resulting in an eerie, supernatural feeling. Sterling naturally suspected the pond was where Stewart had died, especially with all the ghostly activity surrounding the peaceful setting—but who would want to kill an innocent little boy?

The list of suspects was very narrow—in fact, it consisted of one person: Ronald. He alone had something to gain from the child's disappearance. Now, with the boy gone, Lisa would be more willing to become pregnant again.

On the day Stewart went missing at the mall, the police interrogated him for six hours; his story never changed. His whereabouts at the time of the boy's vanishing were corroborated by his trusty butler, Justin. But there was something here, in these watery depths, that wouldn't settle. So here is where the answers must lie.

Even before he had been called onto the case by Lisa, Sterling had followed it closely in the newspaper. He remembered reading that Ronald had hired a truckload of private investigators, hoping that something would break in the case, but it hadn't happened. It was almost as if Stewart vanished in midair. Eventually, the reporters began to speculate that the perpetrator was someone from Ronald's past, which his business dealings had victimized. But there was no hope left now, especially since the kidnappers never requested any ransom.

As he stood gazing out across the pond, listening to the peaceful quiet, only interrupted by the sounds of buzzing insects, in front of him appeared the now-familiar red cardinal, turning its head side to side.

"Hey there, little fellow," Sterling called out to the little bird. After a short time, he began to whistle to the bird. It turned its head side to side, eyeing him curiously. Sterling continued to whistle as the bird hopped about the deck, enjoying the tune. Unexpectedly, it stopped, flew toward the sandy beach near the pond's edge, and began pecking at the muddy soil. It continued jabbing the mud until it made a slight indent. It took a nearby pebble in its beak, dropped it inside the divot, flapped its wings, and flew away.

Sterling wasn't sure what to make of the strange behavior. Was the bird trying to show him something? He soon began to yawn, feeling tired, and glanced down at his wristwatch; it was very late. He decided it was time for bed and returned to the house. As he reached the front door, he heard a car driving quickly up the driveway.

As it came to a stop, Justin exited the vehicle. He glared at Sterling as he ran to open the rear passenger door. Barkley, the family lawyer, stepped out, briefcase in his hand. He sternly walked up to Sterling.

"What in the hell gives you the right to tell Lisa that her son is dead, you stupid bastard!"

Hearing the commotion, Lisa appeared on her balcony.

"Mr. Barkley, that will be enough."

"I'm sorry, Mrs. Howard, but when your husband got your call, he asked me to do something about it. So I agreed to confront this swindler and tell him he's to be gone by morning."

"I'm not willing for Mr. Sterling to leave just yet. He has convinced me that Stewart is dead."

"Excuse me, Mrs. Howard, but that's what I mean. Stewart has been taken by some thugs that want to hurt you and your husband, nothing more. I'm sure the police will find him soon, but you cannot believe this man's charade is playing on you. Please, you must believe me, Mrs. Howard. This charlatan is simply after your money and wants nothing to do with finding your son."

"He is staying, and that is all there is to it, Mr. Barkley.

There is something else that I want you and my husband to understand: Sterling hasn't asked me for one cent! He's here of his own free will. Now goodnight, Mr. Barkley."

Hearing the anger in her voice, the frustrated lawyer walked back to the car. Justin closed the door, turned around, and gave Sterling a look of utter hatred. After they drove away, the smile on Sterling's face couldn't be helped. Seeing the arrogant lawyer being knocked down a couple of pegs was refreshing.

Sterling headed to his room and crawled beneath the sheets to sleep after walking back inside the house. He felt exhausted but set his alarm for 2:12 a.m. His mind drifted; he knew he would soon discover the whereabouts of Stewart's body. The forces at work that held him prisoner were beginning to crumble, and soon they'd give up their secrets. It would not be easy but knowing that Lisa still believed in him was rejuvenating.

Sterling drifted off, thinking of Lisa, and when the alarm sounded, he opened his eyes and reached to shut it off, only to see a knife descending downward, ready to pierce his heart. He instinctively grabbed the arm that held the blade, struggling to push it away. But his attacker was prepared. Sterling deflected the killing blow but the knife sliced his chest, and blood ran down his side as he struggled to stay alive.

Grabbing his attacker's arm with both hands, he slowly pushed him toward the side of the bed in the reddish glow of the alarm clock that still rang out noisily. Sterling could see the smile on the butler's face.

Sterling struggled to kick off his bedsheets to free his legs even as he kept hold of Justin's arm with his right hand. He swung his left arm up and punched Justin in the eye. Justin's head jerked back but his grip on the knife remained strong. Finally freeing his legs from the blankets, Sterling kneed Justin in the stomach, forcing him back and giving

Sterling enough leverage to turn the man facedown on the bed, his knife hand now twisted behind him.

Justin was weakening but not soon enough. He still fought hard. Using the last bit of strength he could muster, Sterling twisted the knife from Justin's hand, and the large man reeled backward, rolling off the bed to stand a few feet away.

Sterling jumped off the bed, the knife now in his hand, expecting to chase Justin. But the man didn't move. He was more than just a butler; he'd probably been used by Ronald before to clean up a mess or two. Now Sterling was the clutter that needed cleaning.

"I know where Stewart's body is hidden!" Sterling said, hoping to distract the man.

Justin stepped back and laughed loudly. "You don't know shit, Sterling, except you're about to meet your maker. When it comes to the brat's body, neither you nor his slut mother will ever find it."

"You're pretty confident for someone who no longer holds the knife. So tell me, Justin, why won't I find Stewart's body?"

Justin slowly began to circle toward Sterling, arms in a fighter's pose. "I've taken care of better than you before," he said, "so I suppose it doesn't matter if you know. You're going to die either way. One of the boulders near the pond is fake. Inside the fiberglass rock is where I put Stewart's body. There's room for you there, too."

He grabbed Sterling's arm and tried to twist the blade from his hand. "There's nothing that you can do about it. When I'm done with you, it will be my pleasure to have you join him." Justin lunged forward, grabbing the knife from Sterling's hand.

Dammit! I let my guard down, Sterling thought, even as he dodged the attack and delivered a back kick to Justin's face, breaking his nose and sending Justin backward into the wall from the impact.

Justin shrugged it off and came at Sterling swinging the knife from side to side. "You're going to die, Sterling."

Calmly, Sterling allowed his attacker to come within striking distance. Then, just as Justin was about to plunge the knife into Sterling's heart, he delivered a punch into Justin's throat. He got up slowly from the floor and flicked on the light switch. Justin flopped to the ground, trying to catch his breath.

Sterling was sure the fight was done. That was his mistake. He walked over to the large man and reached to secure his arms behind his back. Justin grabbed him by his shirt and threw him against the wall. Sterling grunted in pain as Justin jumped to his feet and wrapped his hands around Sterling's throat. The tables had turned; now it was Sterling fighting to breathe.

Tangling with someone trained in various methods of self-defense was foolish at best. Many years ago Sterling reached black belt status, earning his fourth degree in training. The punches and kicks were weapons, just a handful of techniques he could apply from his arsenal. After a crushing blow to any number of weak joints in the human body, Justin would die instantly. Sterling resisted taking that death punch to Justin's heart; he didn't want to be known as a murderer, never a killer taking a human life. This method taught him many years ago by his master was a last-ditch means he could use if all else failed to resist Justin's advances.

I must end this now! This big oaf should be grateful he'd still be alive. Of course, all of Sterling's training was meant to maintain control of any situation. Still, he was growing irritated that he was awakened so unexpectedly and now was in a physical match.

Desperately reaching out for something to aid him, he groped atop the nearby dresser; his hand grasped a Little

League trophy that Stewart had won. Sterling brought it down on Justin's head, and the man's eyes rolled back. He lost his grip on Sterling's throat and collapsed to the floor.

Sterling coughed as he gasped for air. Catching his breath, he rummaged through the boy's toys for something to tie up his attacker. Sterling noticed a game console, ripped the electrical cord from the wall, and bound Justin's hands behind his back. Still panting, he looked around. The small bedroom was in shambles: Cracked plaster on the walls, torn bedclothes, and pieces of Stewart's prized trophy littered the floor.

Sterling felt a sense of relief. He walked downstairs to the main floor of the house. A light glowed in the library. Ronald, obviously drunk, looked up when Sterling walked in.

"I'm surprised to see you here," he said, slurring.

"I bet you are, you bastard!" Walking over to the telephone, he dialed a familiar number. After a couple of rings, he heard a friendly voice on the other end.

"Hello."

"Jack, it's me, Sterling."

"Sterling! What in the world are you doing calling me at this hour?"

"Jack, I need you to get to Howard's residence as quickly as possible. I have solved the Stewart Howard case,"

"What! What do you mean?" Jack said, still half asleep.

"I discovered the murderer, okay? Just get here quickly, please."

"Sure, I'll see you in about an hour!"

"Thank you, Jack."

Hanging up the phone, Sterling looked over at Ronald with disgust.

"I want you to know it was an accident," Ronald stuttered. "I never intended to hurt little Stewart; I just—um—I, it was an accident. I should have never tried to teach him how to swim."

"I'm sure your wife won't see it that way."

"Oh, my wife, well, she won't be awake for several more hours. By the time she wakes, I'll be in Switzerland or someplace that doesn't have an extradition treaty. I gave her a little something to make her sleep."

"Lisa, what did she do to deserve this?" Sterling shook his head in regret.

Taking another swig of Scotch, Ronald yelled.

"Answer me this, how could I tell my wife that it was just an accident? I couldn't help the fact that the boy couldn't swim. I was tired of his weakness and frailties. I decided to teach him to swim as my father taught me. I threw him in the pond and left him there. When I sent Justin to check on him, the boy must have hit his head on the dock or something. Justin found him floating dead."

"You could have told the police if it was an accident!"

"No, too late for that, especially since Justin took the boy's body and hid it from the police. So I made up a story the police would believe. Then I had the landscapers put a small bench where Lisa loves to sit in the evenings. I thought it appropriate that Lisa could be near her son, even though she'd never see him grow to a man."

"You're a complete ass, Ronald," Sterling said, sitting down to watch Ronald until the police arrived. Despite his boast that he would take a plane to Switzerland, he seemed to know it was all over—*or maybe he was just too drunk to move*, Sterling thought tiredly.

Finally, the doorbell rang.

Sterling turned to Ronald. "Well, you'll have plenty of time to think about what you have done while your ass is rotting behind bars."

Walking over to the front door, Sterling quickly opened the door and greeted Jack and the other cops he had brought with him. After explaining what had happened, he went upstairs to check on Lisa. He sat by her bed and watched her sleep peacefully until she finally awakened.

"Sterling? Why are you here?" she said sleepily. "I'm so groggy this morning. Has something more happened? Have you found—?"

"Yes, I know where Stewart's body is located."

"Oh my God. Even though I knew yesterday Stewart must be dead, I still hoped that somehow it wouldn't be true," she cried. "Where is my little boy?"

"He has been closer to you than any of us realized. Do you remember where you like to sit in the evenings, near the pond? Well, close to you were his remains, stuffed inside a fake boulder."

"A boulder—but why? Who did this, Sterling? It couldn't have been strangers."

"I think you know, Lisa."

"Ronald," she said bitterly.

"Yes, with Justin's help."

Sterling wanted to hold, comfort, stay with, and help her through the long days ahead. But it wouldn't work. He knew that. He was the one who had found her son's dead body. He was the one who had discovered her husband's crime.

Quietly, he bent over, gave her a soft kiss, cupping her cheek tenderly, and walked away.

Chapter 3
Who Shot Robert Connelly?

Sterling had just finished another case. A missing husband had been discovered overseas, living another life with another woman. Often the truth isn't what it seems, and most of the time it's not worth knowing But Shanice had been persistent. Once she learned the truth, she hired a lawyer and set about making her husband pay. Sterling understood her reason for ending the marriage. He had sat at breakfast with Shanice; he'd come to like and respect her. She was an excellent mother to her three children, who had begun to call him "Uncle Sterling."

He had developed a soft spot for tiny Ebony, the four-year-old daughter, and the two older boys loved having a man around. He had begun to feel like family, and he hoped he would be able to stay in touch once the case was over. He didn't have any family, just Jack. And the thought of friends who insisted he return for the Thanksgiving holiday made getting into his car to leave Portsmouth, New Hampshire, much more pleasant.

It was a drive of several hours to his home in the city, and Sterling stopped at a small town and gassed up his vehicle. He was tired, and there were menacing clouds overhead; the wind was driving inland from Cape Cod Bay, and the temperature steadily dropped. Thinking that perhaps he should find a place to stay for the night, he pulled away from the station and traveled down the narrow streets of Warwick, Rhode Island, looking for a hotel.

Not far away he found a small, pleasant bed and breakfast. Sterling pulled his black Porsche into the driveway and parked against a painted, white picket fence decorated with the few roses of autumn. Stepping out, he popped open the front compartment, took out a small suitcase, and headed up the short pathway. Sterling came to an ornate front door with a beautiful stained-glass window. Turning the brass doorknob, he walked inside the vestibule and closed the door.

No one was around to greet him. He continued inside toward what appeared to be a drawing-room, paused a moment, and called out.

"Hello, is anyone here?"

Listening for a response, he heard none.

Sterling stood there, checking out the place. He waited a few minutes. Still, no one appeared. The walls were decorated with many shelves displaying an assortment of glass knickknacks of small animals and other collectible figurines of children playing. French Provincial tables showed off crystal vases and art glass abstract centerpieces that looked expensive.

There was an oak table in the center of the room with a white lace tablecloth hanging neatly over all four corners. In the center of the table lay a crystal vase with bright, colorful flowers that looked freshly picked. In the corner of the room sat two overstuffed chairs with white lace doilies covering their backs, looking invitingly comfortable.

An assortment of pictures of various people hung on the walls, including an elderly gentleman fishing at some cabin in the woods. The photograph was black and white and looked as though it could be fifty years old. Another showed the same individual proudly showing off his catch, displayed on a stringer, and smiling brightly. Still, another photo showed a much younger man wrapped his arms around a young woman, both of whom looked happy.

There were more pictures of the two young girls, one with light curly hair and the other a short-haired brunette, on the opposite wall. Both children flashed bright smiles and looked no older than ten years old. These pictures, too, seemed very old and faded but hung on the wall proudly.

Hearing a squeaky door open down the hallway, Sterling returned to the lobby and saw a door opening that he hadn't noticed before. An older woman, whom he guessed to be in her late sixties, stepped out, then turned back around and yelled down to the basement.

"Charlie, I told you that old furnace needs maintenance."

From below came the male's reply, "Yes, ma'am, I'm working on it."

The woman turned around and, seeing Sterling standing there watching the whole affair, greeted him pleasantly.

"Hello, can I help you?"

"Yes, of course. My name is Sterling. I would like a room for the night."

"Of course. It so happens that we have a room available," the woman said with a bright smile.

Closing the door behind her, she walked to a small table in the hallway. Opening up a Registry book, she said, "Excuse me, Mr. Sterling, but how long will you stay with us?"

"Just for one night. I have a pressing matter that I must attend to in the city."

"Oh, that's too bad, Mr. Sterling. You will miss out on seeing our little dinner play. We encourage all our guests to participate. It's a mystery theater, you understand. The name of the play is called 'Who shot Mr. Connelly?'"

"A dinner play? That sounds intriguing."

"It's based on a true story in this house that happened so many years ago. Mr. Connelly is my deceased brother-in-law; his first name was Richard. The story goes that he arrived home unannounced late one evening from a business trip. It was storming that night, with the rain and wind blowing violently outside. He had forgotten his keys and couldn't have gotten inside without waking everyone. But somehow he gained entry, though no one knows exactly how; the home had been completely locked tight for the evening, and there was no way inside except through the front door."

"Yes, that does sound a bit mysterious."

"Well, the best we could figure out was that he magically appeared in the drawing-room. As he stood there dripping wet and shaking off the water from his jacket, without warning a single shot was fired by a mysterious gunman who was never discovered. The bullet went right through Mr. Connelly's heart and lodged in the nearby wall. If you look across from where you are standing, you will see a small hole where the bullet entered the plaster wall. That bullet is immortalized behind plastic."

"Excuse me, but that sounds morbid. You made a mystery theater about Richard's murder?"

"Why, yes, Mr. Sterling. They never caught his murderer and couldn't find any clues on why he was shot. All they did find were his muddy footprints that led to the front of the house. There should have been other footprints from the murderer, but there weren't any! There is something else. The front door was completely locked with a chain across the jamb. So the real mystery was how

Richard got inside, especially since he wasn't due to arrive home until the following day."

"So you're saying that the police never found the murderer or the weapon used in the killing, right? Perhaps he was the sort of man who had enemies?"

"No, not Richard. He was loved by his wife and the people of our town. Along with community projects, he arranged to help the homeless and needy. He was a generous man who fought for equality."

"Hmm, well, someone had a dislike for the man!"

"Yes, I suppose you're right. However, when his body was discovered the following day, his shoes had no trace of mud on them. Nonetheless, his muddy footprints were on the outside porch in front of the house. Plus there is something else: He had a receipt from a local hotel in his right coat pocket and a hundred dollars in his other pocket, which no one could explain. Why did he have a receipt for a hotel if he was planning to come home? And he never carried that much cash with him."

Just then an older woman appeared from a back room. She walked with a cane; she didn't look up or notice Sterling standing there but continued walking past, apparently motivated by her personal agenda.

"Mr. Sterling, this is my older sister Hannah, or Mrs. Connelly."

Stopping briefly to look up, she calmly said, "Hello, Mr. Sterling," Then she walked into the next room and disappeared.

Turning back around, Sterling stared at the woman behind the counter as if looking for an explanation.

Seeing his expression, she softly replied, "I'm sorry, Mr. Sterling, for my sister's rudeness. She hasn't been the same since losing her husband some fifty years ago. I hope you will understand."

"Yes, of course. About the room?"

"Oh yes. Let's see, the total will be a hundred and ten dollars for the night. Will you be paying with a credit card or cash, Mr. Sterling?"

"With cash," Sterling responded, taking out his wallet and paying the woman.

She gave him a room key marked 208 and explained that his room would be at the top of the stairs, the second room from the end.

"I also wanted to say that we serve dinner promptly at six o'clock, Mr. Sterling."

He thanked her and started walking away. But before he got very far, she called out.

"If you need anything else, Mr. Sterling, call down to the front desk and ask for me. My name is Annabelle."

"Thank you, Annabelle."

Walking upstairs to the second floor and down the hall, Sterling counted the rooms and came to bedroom 208 where he unlocked the door and stepped inside. He first noticed a large, soft bed in the middle of the room and an oak dresser with a marble top positioned in front of the window. The drawers were decorated with white ceramic knobs; he guessed the dresser was over a hundred years old.

Setting down his suitcase on the bed, he reached for his wallet and searched through the many business cards he had kept inside. Finally, toward the back of his wallet, he found the particular card he was looking for, dialed the number, and waited for someone to pick it up. Suddenly, a voice recorder came on. A woman's voice explained that she was busy and couldn't come to the phone. Not wanting to leave a message, Sterling hung up.

Afterward, he unpacked his clothes, putting them away in the antique dresser. As he finished he heard a ringing bell from downstairs, telling all the houseguests that dinner was now served.

As Sterling walked down the hallway, the delicious

smell of dinner filled the entire house. When he appeared in the dining room, he was greeted by other guests. Sitting at the table, a lady to his far right introduced herself as Lynn Macbeth, a reddish-haired woman around her late forties, wearing expensive jewelry. A gentleman with thinning gray hair wearing a plaid shirt and bright red bow tie to his left stood up to shake Sterling's hand, introducing himself as Marty Johnson, a salesman from Detroit who sold plastic wheel covers to the automotive factories. Next to him was an older gentleman named Carter Townsend, a retired air force master chief, and his wife, Peggy.

She smiled and said, "I'm just a dull housewife and mother of four. Nothing special there."

Just then Annabelle came into the room accompanied by a young Hispanic girl carrying a large steaming bowl of homemade stew, which she sat on a placeholder in the center of the table. Annabelle's sister slowly followed behind, bringing a loaf of homemade bread and butter.

Afterward, taking her place at the head of the table, Hannah sat down while Annabelle sat next to Sterling. Hannah eyed everyone, then asked if anyone would care to say grace. When no one volunteered, staring at one another with somewhat puzzled looks, Hannah took the initiative, bowed her head, and began praying.

"Thank you, good Lord, for this bounty that we are about to receive. We thank you for your enduring love and provisions this day."

Everyone joined in with a resounding shout of "Amen," which Annabelle repeated a moment later. She then stood, opened the serving dish's lid, and grabbed ahold of the spoon. The steam from the stew filled the air with a mouth-watering aroma.

Once everyone's bowl was filled and the bread passed around, Annabelle said, "Dig in, everyone, before it gets cold."

Silence reigned in the room as everyone enjoyed the dinner.

Halfway through dinner Lynn Macbeth spoke up. "Mr. Sterling, what do you do for a living, if you don't mind me asking?"

After swallowing, Sterling looked up from the table. "I'd like to clarify something: First, my name is not Mr. Sterling. I'd prefer it if you called me Sterling. My actual name is not important to anyone; what brings me here is a desperate need for peaceful rest for a night and nothing more. As far as what I do for a living, all I can say is that I will soon be helping a family find their missing daughter."

"Oh! Are you a private detective then, Sterling?" Lynn asked.

"No, not really. I'm what you'd call a psychic detective. What I mean is that I communicate with the living and sometimes the dead. When I enter a conscious dream state, I can see into another world where clues are visible to my trained eye."

"You do!" an astonished Mrs. Townsend spoke up. "What does that mean exactly, Sterling, that part about communicating with the dead? Let me ask: Are you talking to the dead now?"

"No, Mrs. Townsend. I'm talking to the living. I'm talking to you, aren't I?"

A silence followed, and then everyone at the table laughed.

"Yes, of course. I knew that I'd seen your face before," Marty interjected. "It was in all the newspapers,"

Rising from his chair, he pointed his finger at Sterling and said, "You're the one that solved the Howard case. The one involving the missing eight-year-old boy. I knew it! I kept staring at you, thinking I'd seen your face before."

He sat back down, feeling proud of himself for his brilliant deduction.

Everyone's curiosity at the dining table was aroused; they stopped eating and stared at Sterling with great interest, whispering to one another. He tried ignoring their stares. Taking another bite of his food, he chewed it and slowly swallowed. It was painfully evident that he was the only one eating. He paused for a moment and looked around the table at all the gleaming faces looking back at him.

"Why not have the Mystery Theater tonight instead of tomorrow?" Lynn said excitedly. "Now that we have such an honored guest in our midst."

Everyone agreed, thinking it was a brilliant idea—everyone except Sterling, who only wanted to finish his meal. He looked at Annabelle for help; she only shrugged her shoulders and continued to eat her meal.

STERLING HAD NOT AGREED to be a part of the Mystery Theater that evening. But regardless of his wishes, excitement filled the air. A homemade cheesecake was brought out, along with coffee for those who needed to stay awake for the midnight show. A few hours before the show started, all the women left the dining table to freshen up, leaving the men to themselves.

Annabelle and the young Hispanic girl began clearing the dinner dishes from the dining table. Sterling spoke up.

"That meal was very delicious. All that's needed is a small glass of timely aged port and a cigar."

Annabelle held the empty stew bowl and threw a kitchen towel over her shoulder. "That's a superb idea, Sterling. In times past our father and his guests would enjoy a brandy and a smoke in the library after dinner."

"What are we waiting for? Let's go and partake, gentleman," said Mr. Townsend, leading the way to the library.

Annabelle directed them to a small cart near a tall bookshelf when they walked inside the elegant room. There sat a crystal decanter filled with some aged brandy. Next to the decanter sat a small humidor. Sterling opened the lid and found a variety of cigars, some Churchill, Robusto, and Corona. Taking a Churchill, he lifted it to his ear and twisted it between his fingers to test its freshness.

Pleased with his choice, Sterling turned to Annabelle and said, "Would you care to join us?"

"No, thank you. Some dishes need cleaning back in the kitchen."

Marty Johnson was eager for a much-needed smoke and hurried to the small cart. He promptly lifted the lid and picked out a large Robusto from Ecuador. Mr. Townsend chose a similar cigar, lit the tightly packed tobacco leaf, and blew out a thick swirling smoke that clouded the room in a rich aroma.

Sitting in the chair next to the fireplace, Sterling turned to Mr. Townsend. "If you don't mind me asking, where did you serve in the military?"

"Sterling, you can call me Carter."

"Carter, it is. So where did you serve? I was only curious because some friends of mine, serving in the military, found themselves in the Arabian Desert, riding in a tank, going straight to Kuwait," Sterling announced.

"Yes, good old Kuwait. I've been there. Wherever there was a need for a tank, I was there to the rescue."

"Hey, I need a drink. Would anyone else care for one?" Marty asked.

"Splendid idea, Marty, I'll have one," Carter answered.

"Make that three," Sterling said.

Returning to the small cart, Marty took three glasses and began to pour. When he finished, he handed one to Sterling and said, "Are you really a, what did you call it? A psychic detective?"

"I'm not sure what your interpretation of a psychic is, but all I can say is that I can hear the dead speaking at times and see things left behind by the dead. I don't use a crystal ball or smoke and mirrors, nothing like that," Sterling explained.

"Sounds weird to me, if you don't mind me saying so," Marty announced, handing a glass of brandy to Carter.

Then, taking one himself, he toasted to their health. Having clinked their glasses together, everyone took a sip, and Carter commented that it went down smoother than a mint julep in July.

The men discussed the usual topics for the next few hours, from American troop deployment overseas to past wars. Sterling grew quiet as if lost in thought.

Marty slapped him on the shoulders and asked, "What's up, Sterling? You having a psychic nightmare or something?" He laughed, greatly amused with himself.

"No, sorry, you must excuse me. I find myself somewhere else; I cannot say where. It's as if a memory was awakened, and I travel to someplace dark and menacing." Finishing his drink, he admitted, "It's not pleasant; I hate that part of the spiritual traverse. You never know where you're going. It's more of a curse than a blessing,"

The other men weren't sure what to say—it was a subject as strange and unknown to them as the grave itself.

Seeing death firsthand in Kuwait, Carter was no stranger to seeing blown apart bodies and the gross aftermath of a tank battle. The Grim Reaper had passed him nearby on serval occasions when a car bomb ignited at the head of the column he was traveling in or other times in his tour when overhead rockets began falling from the sky. But this man, this Sterling, whom Carter had just met, announced he often traveled to the other dimension. It gave him the creeps, and he shuddered as a result.

Oblivious to Sterling's announcement, perhaps the alcohol-infused brain couldn't appreciate the concept, Marty downed his last drink of brandy and asked, "Would anyone else care for another?

"Sure," Carter replied. "I'm not going anywhere else this evening."

Annabelle called Marty to join her in the hallway, and a few minutes later he reappeared in a raincoat, which looked strange since it wasn't raining outside. He excitedly announced to Sterling and Carter that he was asked to play the part of Richard Connelly that evening.

"I can't believe my luck!"

Adjusting his coat and hat, he added, "It was Annabelle who asked me. Perhaps it was that I had the starring role in Romeo and Juliet in high school."

A simple "No" was heard from Carter as he sipped on his brandy, trying not to encourage the man but doing his best not to break out in laughter.

"I'm so excited that we're doing this tonight!" said Marty. "I've been studying the brochure. These two sisters have been performing this play for years."

"I wonder why I've never heard of the dinner play before?" Sterling replied.

"Not sure, but I must be off to practice my lines—see ya soon." Marty disappeared from the room.

Sterling looked over at Carter, who was snickering.

"Marty, the starring role, I would have never guessed that, would you?"

"Nope. I would have never guessed that in a million years," Carter said with a grin.

Lynn burst into the room, wearing a brightly colored red silk outfit and filling the room with an overpowering fragrance that resembled roses blooming in the spring. Stopping in front of Sterling, using her low, sensual voice, she asked, "Sir, would you please be a darling and pour me a drink?"

"Of course, tell me what type of drink you would like. After all I cannot read everyone's mind," Sterling answered with a laugh.

"It doesn't matter to me. A simple brandy, straight up, or perhaps whiskey on the rocks."

"Sure, ma'am, right away."

A moment later after taking her drink, Lynn tasted it. "Where exactly is this play going to be held?"

Carter spoke up. "According to the story Richard Connelly was shot in the hallway leading to the drawing-room. I imagine Marty will have to be shot there for this to be authentic. I suspect the show should begin soon. I had better get upstairs and get my wife before she misses out."

"Brilliant idea, Carter. I'm sure you wouldn't want to miss the performance," Sterling responded, then watched him disappear upstairs.

Sipping his brandy, Sterling looked around the room at the unique objects. He was sure that they hadn't been moved in years. Probably everything was the same as it had been on that fateful night when a man was murdered in the hallway. A few moments later he stood, walked out of the library, and moseyed out into the hall.

Closing his eyes, he began to imagine that faithful night and what had happened to Mr. Connelly. According to folklore or at least what Annabelle had told him, a harsh rainstorm had appeared that evening, explaining why no one heard the gunshot in the room. A clap of thunder outside masked the shot.

Walking into the drawing-room, Sterling strolled over to where the bullet had entered the wall. Using his imagination, he envisioned the details, not actually knowing what occurred—only pure speculation on his part. Without warning the clock on the wall sounded eleven resounding gongs from its brass working mechanism, breaking his concentration.

It's that late already. Where did the evening go?

Sterling returned to the library without feeling any

spiritual connection into the mystical world and sat in one of the overstuffed chairs where everyone was to meet. After a short wait he was joined by all the guests and Hannah.

Without warning the lights in the house were dimmed, then the glow of a single candle being carried by Annabelle appeared from the hallway. She was dressed in an outfit that seemed to be from the fifties.

Walking into the drawing-room with the lit candle, she stopped in the middle of the room and stared blankly into space. Then, as if in a trance, she placed the candle on the nearby coffee table, took out a piece of old, worn paper, and began reading aloud.

"The story I'm about to tell you is true, and I must warn you all: Many of you could find this frightening. This story involves an innocent man who died mysteriously. It all happened one stormy night many years ago."

At the precise moment she uttered those words, a commotion was heard in the hallway. Everyone jumped and ran to see what had caused the disturbance. There stood a man dressed in a raincoat. Everyone knew it to be Marty, with water dripping off his overcoat, which Sterling found humorous.

Dripping wet, he carried a briefcase and wore a hat that looked soaked as well.

Standing there for a brief moment, Annabelle continued reading from the small piece of paper: "Mr. Connelly came home unexpectedly and somehow got into the house unannounced. While he stood in the dark hallway, the storm outside raged on. Unknown to him, someone was lurking in the shadows. Someone was waiting to shoot him dead. Somehow this stranger knew that he would arrive at this precise time and waited to strike a fatal blow."

While Marty stood in the hallway, still dripping wet, a character dressed all in black appeared from around the corner and stood in the entryway. This person drew a gun and fired a single shot at Marty's body. Unfortunately, hearing the gunshot, though it was just a blank, upset Hannah, who had repeatedly endured the replaying of this tragic event over the years. Sterling guessed the assailant was played by Maria, the staff worker, hidden under a dark bedsheet.

Sterling noticed that she could barely watch the drama unfold. She closed her eyes at the precise moment her husband was hit by the bullet from the assailant's gun. Annabelle's voice then broke the still silence by reading the final words from her paper: "The killer escaped that night into the darkness, never to be discovered."

Observing Marty in character, he seemed to be excellently playing a dead guy; he hadn't moved the entire time but was still lying on the floor.

Carter, fearing the worst, walked over to check on him. The smell of alcohol on his breath was overpowering.

Marty jumped up from the floor. As he got closer, he shouted, "Not to fear, it's me, alive and well."

The lights came back on, and jubilant applause broke out among the guests. Everyone cheered Marty, telling him that he was the best-looking dead guy anyone had ever seen and rushed over to pat him on the back for his exceptional performance.

Sterling and Carter looked at each other without saying a word, sharing the same thought: How hard is it to lie on the floor playing a dead guy, anyway?

Sterling turned and noticed Hannah, who remained speechless throughout the performance. He walked over and expressed his regret that she had to endure the terrible memory of losing her husband again.

Looking up with teary eyes, Hannah responded, "It's all right; it doesn't bother me too much." Her face revealed the sadness that still haunted her soul.

"Still, it cannot be pleasant to watch," Sterling argued.

"No, but it keeps the memory of my beloved Richard alive. Call me a stupid old woman, but I still believe that Robert was coming home early to surprise me with a second honeymoon with all that cash he had in his pocket. You see, Mr. Sterling, certain things were never the same between us after losing our first child. But we tried to make it work. When I heard that Robert had been shot, I couldn't believe it was true. I wished I could have been there that night to be surprised to see him home early, but I was called away to visit a close friend who was dying from pneumonia."

Surprisingly, more cheers were ringing behind them, making it difficult to hear, but Sterling focused on Hannah.

"Can we return to the library and continue the conversation?" he asked.

Agreeing, she followed Sterling to the library.

Once there, she spoke again. "After all these years Robert's death is still a mystery to us. I could never figure out why he didn't telegram me that he was coming home. He worked in advertising as a business executive and often traveled to Chicago and New York. That week before his death, he acted strangely. He spent many days in town working late and would get a hotel room instead of catching the train home, which seemed odd to me. But that was Robert, I suppose," Hannah surmised, as though she sought answers after all these years.

Having approached silently, Annabelle appeared next to her sister. "Well, Mr. Sterling, what did you think of our little mystery?"

"I can see that the killing makes no sense. But I have learned that the answers to most mysteries lie in front of your very nose if you are willing to see them. I don't have the answers that you seek, only more questions. But I have a curious awareness that allows me to smell out the truth—at times—though perhaps this isn't one of those times, I'm afraid. Sorry, I don't have any free time to spend on your mystery. I must leave in the morning."

"Mr. Sterling, I hope you will consider staying for breakfast. Our delicious homemade French toast is the rave all around town, you know," Annabelle said.

Hannah, looking tired, nodded her head in agreement. "Yes, you should consider having breakfast before you leave us, Mr. Sterling. Perhaps there is something that you might uncover before you leave."

The way she asked made him feel compelled to stay a little longer, as if she was begging for him to solve the mystery of her husband's death.

"I cannot make any promises, but I will see by morning, which is already upon us. Sorry, I must retire to bed; otherwise, I will be of no use to anyone, including myself."

Marty arrived in the library, holding another drink in his hand. He slapped Sterling on the back. "Well, Sterling, old boy, what did you think of my performance? Tell me, didn't I seem dead to you?" he asked, slurring his words and spilling his drink all over his damp raincoat.

Yes, dead drunk. While Sterling grinned at the thought, he kept his words polite. "Yes, it was quite a performance, almost worthy of an Oscar."

Lynn Macbeth appeared next, gripping a cigarette between her lips and taking another sip of her whiskey. "Sterling, did you figure out who killed poor Robert Connelly? I was hoping you would have said the killer was the butler," she laughed. "I was disappointed to hear that you are retiring to bed. Why is that, Sterling? Haven't you been able to speak to the ghost of Robert Connelly?" she said snidely.

Rather than respond to her offensive comments, Sterling turned to the others and explained: "Ghosts don't just appear when you want them to. Truthfully, they stay for such a short time that you would miss them if you didn't know what signs they left behind. Besides, alcohol deadens your senses to the point that even if a ghost walked in front of your face, you wouldn't know it." Sterling walked away, leaving everyone to ponder his words.

"Sterling, why are you going to bed now?" Marty asked, his slurred words almost incomprehensible. "I thought we would have a séance after the mystery performance. Finally, we'd discover who killed Robert Connelly."

Sterling stopped and turned around. "I didn't say nor did I imply that we were going to have such a thing, Marty. Besides, before long I'm sure you'll see a ghost in the shape of pink elephants."

Hannah surprised Sterling. "Why can't we have a séance? I would love to commune with Robert to learn what happened to him."

Sterling looked at her with compassion. "Hannah, in the spiritual world one doesn't always get the answers to the questions they seek. Sometimes you're better off not knowing the truth because it can be too painful to hear."

"I understand, but I must know what happened to my husband." Looking away, Hannah began to cry. "It's been so long, and soon I'm going to leave this cold world. Anyway, what harm is there in learning the truth, Sterling? Can you do this for me?"

"Knowing the truth can be painful at times. Ignorance is bliss." Looking at Hannah's swollen blue eyes, he conceded to her demands. "Yes. I can try, but I will not guarantee that it will work or that I can find the answer to what is hidden. But for you I will try."

Sterling walked back toward the dining room without saying anything else and was soon followed by the others.

When Carter and his wife Peggy saw the small crowd coming down the hallway, Carter called out, "What's going on? Did one of you guys find Robert Connelly's ghost or something?"

Marty, swishing his drink everywhere, excitedly

shouted, "No, better than that. Mr. Sterling has agreed to have a séance!"

Carter turned to his wife and commented, "I didn't think he would do it!"

"What do you mean?"

"Well, earlier we had a chance to talk. Sterling gave me the impression that he hated communing with the dead. He said that every time he goes into a trance and communicates with the deceased he travels to places that would scare a normal person to death."

"Hmm, I wonder why he agreed to do it?" Peggy responded.

Suddenly, Annabelle turned to her sister and said, "Listen to me, I don't feel this is such a good idea. Some things in life you're better off not knowing!"

"You, most of all, must know how I have suffered all these years," Hannah replied. "Tonight I shall have my answer. I shall discover who killed my husband."

The clock on the wall announced thirty minutes past the midnight hour. It took a short time for the preparations to begin. First, a circular table was needed. Carter and his wife removed the china dinner plates and silverware off the dining table, gently stacking them on the floor.

"Please be careful—those plates once belonged to our grandmother—good Lord, they must be over a hundred years old!" Hannah announced.

Her pleas were partly ignored; immediately, the dishes were stacked haphazardly on the floor, along with the expensive silverware.

Marty staggered into the room. "Tell me, you guys need my help?"

"Yes, Marty, please grab one end of this table, and let's move it to the library," Carter said.

Just as they struggled to move the mahogany table, Peggy quickly grabbed ahold of the lace tablecloth, folded it neatly, and placed it atop the plates. With a mighty heave, Carter and Marty carried the table down the hallway to the library; Peggy and Annabelle brought chairs. Soon there were enough chairs to accompany all the guests. Next, upon the table, a dark-colored tablecloth was spread out. Then Sterling ordered everyone out of the room except Annabelle.

Turning to her, he asked, "Tell me, do you have a large candle?"

"You bet. I know the perfect one."

Disappearing from the room, Annabelle soon reappeared carrying a single white candle housed within a decorative crystal. Per Sterling's orders, she placed it in the center of the table and stood nearby to see if something else was needed. She called to the guests, waiting anxiously in the hallway to come back inside. When they trickled in, they saw Sterling sitting at the table. His eyes were closed as if meditating. Each attendee felt nervous in anticipation: They would soon be contacting the dead. Was it morally correct to search out the departed for answers to those questions that were buried and forgotten? No, probably not. Regardless, the deceased had the answers to those questions that many were willing to ask, and tonight was no exception.

Although none would ever suspect Lynn of having a debilitating fear of what lies beyond the curtain, she did have a secret she had kept for many years. With any luck that secret should remain concealed in the cheap coffin she had buried her mother inside. She had stolen money from her dying mother. Now she worried that her mother's ghost would arrive at the party and tell everyone what a selfish daughter she had been.

Most of her mother's estate had been sold to buy Lynn a new expensive Mercedes; *she deserved it*, she thought. After all she had been the one to call a cab to come and pick up her mother for her doctor's appointments, not Ronny, her selfish brother who complained about how their mother was treated. No, she deserved every dime she took.

No surprise, the servant girl Maria was not the least interested in sticking around for the séance. She seemed superstitious, looking back to be sure no one or thing was following her. She informed Annabelle that she had dishes to clean in the kitchen and left the room in a hurry.

Everyone chose a seat and quickly sat down with the table centered in the room. Soon the excitement rose as many guests expressed their fears of what would happen next.

Suddenly, Sterling opened his eyes and asked Annabelle to light the candle. Next, he announced to everyone, "Now it is time to begin. But before we move forward, I must warn you that I have no way of knowing who will speak or what they will say. You have to stay focused on my voice as I alone will direct us where we will go. We are about to visit a place of utter darkness where no light can penetrate. All of you must clear your mind of this present time we inhabit. We will all travel mentally, back in time, to this exact place many years ago. Now please take hold of the hand of the person beside you. Close your eyes, and clear your minds. You must imagine this house, not as it is now but over fifty years ago. Try to remember that stormy night when Robert was murdered and the sounds of the thunder clapping above."

Sterling's voice grew low and soothing. Around the table everyone sat quietly and concentrated on the past. Sterling sat with Hannah on one side and Annabelle on the other. The rest of the seating arrangements were of no importance; he wanted to connect with the actual persons he felt were involved somehow. Though, as yet, he wasn't sure what would develop. Still, he knew the truth must come out.

Sterling's meditation technique allowed his body to relax, and he focused on the pictures on the wall, the gentleman fishing, and the two young girls playing together. Somewhere there was something hidden within their lives that they had never faced, a secret never told or brought to light. Behind the smiling faces here within these walls was the truth of what happened to Robert. Was it a shady business adventure or perhaps something the father had done to a neighbor? What motives led to Mr. Connelly's death? Sterling would try his best to reveal it.

While everyone's attention focused on an imaginary storm raging outside, Sterling asked the keepers of the spiritual world to allow their secrets to be brought to light and to loosen the bonds that held the truth about Robert Connelly's murder.

Of course, all of this was for show; Sterling had no intentions of inviting a ghostly spirit to the party. Most séances were more than scams devised to rob old ladies of their money. To Sterling, the truth of the murder would be discovered by examining the clues left behind, not from listening to a dead spirit.

Now, as everyone eagerly waited for some omen from the other world, the room grew deathly quiet—so much so that all seated at the table imagined themselves traveling to another world where death resides.

As Sterling led their thoughts to an event that happened many years ago, he directed them to imagine traveling back in time, back to that fateful night when Robert was murdered. Each one began to imagine the dark hallway just beyond, with the sounds of heavy rain outside. Slowly, they began to see the soaking wet image of Robert Connelly standing in the hallway.

Sterling drew them an imaginary picture. "See a soaking wet Robert standing in the hallway. Imagine the feeling of being cold and wet. Bright lightning flashes outside, and the thunder booms afterward."

Using the power of persuasion, he added, "Now imagine for the moment the house is still and quiet, no one is awake, and all are sleeping snugly in their beds."

With everyone's imagination under Sterling's control,

they concentrated on Robert appearing in the dark hallway. They all could see him in his raincoat stumbling about the darkness, with only the occasional lightning strike outside to offer any light.

Sterling left everyone to their imagination; he had his own agenda and began to travel back to that fateful night. In his mind he traced the projectile's ballistic trajectory, backward from the plastered wall and through the darkness toward where the shot was fired.

As he concentrated Sterling saw the smoking barrel of the gun used in the murder. The reddish light that came from the powder burns temporarily lit the room. In the unexpected brightness he saw a much younger Annabelle standing in the hallway, holding the gun in her hand. Annabelle had shot her brother-in-law. The reason why? It was unknown to him, but now the mystery of who shot Robert Connelly was solved.

As the group focused on the image of Robert, their eyes closed. Sterling stared back at an anxious Annabelle; his expression said it all.

The still quiet was shattered.

"Sterling, I don't see shit!" yelled Marty.

The mood broken, Hannah turned to Sterling. "Sterling, tell me, did you see my Robert or anything? Please tell me."

Sterling continued staring at Annabelle and answered, "I'm sorry, Hannah. I wasn't able to connect with Robert as I had hoped. Perhaps if Marty's sudden outburst didn't break our concentration or if we had a little more time. But it's getting late, and I must get some sleep."

"You see that! I didn't think he could contact the dead," Lynn said scornfully, relieved that her dead mother's ghost had not arrived. "Sterling, I think you're lucky sometimes at finding out how people have been murdered. I don't believe you have any special powers or abilities. You're nothing but a charlatan, and if you had asked me, I would have said no, don't have this stupid séance and build up the hopes of this poor woman who wants to know about the man that killed her husband."

As someone turned on the light switch, Sterling remained sitting in his chair, annoyed by Lynn's disbelief. "Maybe you're right, Lynn. Maybe I'm not who people say I am. But if I am indeed that person, may I suggest that you not take any plane trips this year? That is all I'm going to say."

Turning to the others in the room, he added, "Good night."

He rose to his feet and left the room, leaving everyone to wonder if what he had said to Lynn was true or not.

The following morning Sterling rose early and packed his bag. He quietly left his room. Walking down the squeaking stairs, he continued toward the front door and prepared to walk out when a female voice addressed him from within the darkness.

"I never wanted to kill Robert, but he deserved it."

Sterling set his bag down and walked back toward the dining area, stopping in the doorway. Sterling looked behind him; Annabelle was drinking a cup of coffee in the dining area. She wore the same clothing the night before, looking like she'd been up all night.

"Robert—he deserved it," Annabelle repeated.

Sterling looked at the crying woman with sympathy and asked, "Why?"

Annabelle didn't look up and said, "He deserved to die, that bastard." She looked up. "Behind my sister's back Robert continually raped me. I couldn't bring myself to tell Hannah. You see, Mr. Sterling, I love my sister dearly. I want you to believe me when I tell you that Robert was no Prince Charming. I begged him to stop and leave me alone but he wouldn't. My sister never knew what he was doing to me. But when the time came that she had to visit her sick friend, I knew that I would put an end to his raping me once and for all."

"I must ask you: Are you sure you want to admit to murder, Annabelle?"

"Last night I saw the truth in your eyes that you discovered the killer was me. I knew how you reacted afterward; you couldn't keep your eyes off me."

"Perhaps you're right. It is the real reason I'm leaving so early. Otherwise, I'll be tempted to put Lynn in her place and admit that I did discover the truth."

"Well, be that as it may, you should know that my sister and I are very close. I beg you, Mr. Sterling, please don't tell Hannah. I cannot have you telling her the truth. I don't believe she could handle the truth if it were told to her."

"I see."

Annabelle stared into her coffee cup, then back at Sterling. "That night Robert came home and tried to get into my bedroom while I was asleep. When I woke I saw him struggling to open my bedroom window. He was determined to get inside and demanded that I open the window at once. He pushed it up and leaned in, telling me it was time to play. I raced into the hallway, hoping to escape him, but he was too fast and cornered me in the drawing room.

"Thankfully, my father and our servant Mrs. Barmen were sound sleepers and didn't hear the commotion downstairs. My mother had passed away from pneumonia the winter before. Otherwise, my father would have shot Robert himself. Robert and I fought that night as I tried to keep his dirty hands from touching me."

"No one should suffer as you did," Sterling responded in his compassionate voice.

"My father had a handgun—I knew where he kept it. I got to his desk and pulled it out. I tried desperately to stop Robert from raping me. Maybe once he saw the gun, I thought he would become frightened and leave me alone. I was hoping to scare him away." Tears ran down her cheeks.

Sterling, not sure what to say, remained speechless.

"I got as far as the hallway and looked back; he was almost upon me. I was desperate to get away from him and turned and fired a single shot. Robert fell dead on the floor. When I realized what I had done, I became frightened, and I wanted to run out of the house but I knew I couldn't. Instead, I went to my bedroom and cleaned up any trace of Robert entering my room. Then I returned to his body, took his shoes, slipped them on my feet, tracked his muddy footprints all over the front porch, and locked the door tightly. Next, I cleaned the mud off his shoes and put them on his feet. The rain outside erased any footprints he left behind, trying to get inside my bedroom window. Afterward, I cleaned up all the floors in the hallway and the drawing-room and any trace of him having ever been inside the house. Then I crawled back into my bed as though nothing had happened.

All these years I have hidden the truth from my sister. Besides this something else that would have been hard to explain to my family was how I was three months pregnant with Robert's child. When I told him the news, he laughed at me. I suppose that's why he had over a hundred dollars in his pocket—for me to take care of the problem."

"Annabelle, I don't know what to say. The horror you have suffered should not have happened to anyone," Sterling announced.

"No, you're right, sad to say. But the stress of possibly being caught by the police or the regret of shooting Robert dead caused me to have a miscarriage. By the time I got to visit a doctor in another town, someone who wouldn't know my family, the doctor told me I would no longer have children because of the damage caused by the last pregnancy. I was devastated; you must believe me. My only chance at a normal life was shattered so I never married. Thanks to Robert, I could never get pregnant again, and no man would want to marry a barren woman, not in those days."

Sterling saw Annabelle's relief now that she was free of the pain and guilt she had bottled up for all these years. Confessing her story made her appear brighter, no longer sad.

After another sip of coffee, she said, "Well, here we are. Now you know it all. The sad truth. Tell me, what do you intend to do with it, Sterling."

He looked at the broken woman who had suffered so many years in secret and said, "What would the truth serve now? Let Hannah live with the notion that Robert was a good loving husband. I cannot see any reason not to let her believe otherwise." Then he drew closer and said, "As far as I'm concerned, I don't believe that throwing a woman in prison for being tormented and raped is the right thing to do. Live the rest of your days in peace. You have nothing to fear from me."

Sterling picked up his bag and walked out the door.

When he reached his car the clouds above rushed across the sky, signaling a storm was on its way. *We might be getting some rain. Wouldn't that be great; it will fit my mood perfectly.* After opening the trunk of his car, he placed his bag inside and closed the lid. A few droplets appeared, and he quickly jumped inside and started his Porsche.

As he waited for his car to warm up, he noticed something above him. Looking up at the second-floor bedroom window, he saw Lynn Macbeth looking down at him. Her expression was one of doubt and second-guessing. Of course, he couldn't read minds but she had to be wondering if it was wise to be taking any trips in the next year. Looking up, Sterling smiled.

Putting his car into gear, he backed out of the driveway. As he pulled away, he looked again at Lynn's window; she was gone. He turned down Broadway and drove for another mile, traveling to the interstate. When he stopped at the busy intersection, he noticed a proudly advertised billboard: "Next time you stay in Providence, MA, visit the Connelly Bed and Breakfast. Be sure to see the Mystery Theater to discover who shot Mr. Connelly."

Seeing the sign, Sterling laughed loudly and thought, *I already know who shot that bastard.* He shoved his car in gear and drove away.

Chapter 4
The Murder of April Humphry

The day was warm as fluffy clouds filled the sky, and the sun would occasionally appear overhead as a small group of people gathered at a park. The shade provided by the trees was a welcome relief from the penetrating sunrays overhead.

Susan Bernstein turned to Sterling. "When I see the girls playing the game of tag, it reminds me of when I was a little girl. Back then I had a friend named April Humphry. She and I played similar games, well past dark. She ran away from home and never returned. I still miss her."

Hearing this, Sterling closed his eyes, momentarily distracted by a vision of something that happened long ago. Then he said, "April Humphry was murdered. Her killer is still alive."

"Are you sure?" Susan gasped. "They never found her body; everyone suspected she eloped with that Marine she was dating. No one has seen her since."

"Yes," Sterling replied, turning to her as if he had just seen a ghost. "I saw the murderer."

Overcome with emotion, Susan sobbed, then said,

"Please tell me where I can find that bastard."

"I cannot be sure. However, you must understand this will take some concentration and prodigious resolve. All I did was concentrate on your friend; I'm not sure if it's because of your proximity to my physical being, or..." He paused. "it's because she's reaching out to you, her friend? Regardless, we must arrange a time to meet."

"Sterling, just tell me the place and time. I'll be there; you have my word."

"All right, I'll let you know. When we meet, please bring something that belonged to April if you can."

"Yes, I do have something. The night April disappeared she forgot her sweater back at my house. I just never had a desire to get rid of it. It's a small pink sweater, of no real importance to anyone except me," she answered, her words filled with emotion.

"Please bring it along, Susan. I need to see it. I'm sorry but I have to rush. Will you please tell everyone I said goodbye?"

"Certainly."

Watching Sterling leave, she approached her friend Barbara and said, "Sterling had to run. He wanted me to tell you that he'll talk to you later."

"Sterling is leaving? That's too bad. I made his favorite dessert, a banana cream cake. You know we couldn't have done it without him, could we, Susan?"

"No, you're right, and I have to go as well. I'm sorry."

"I thought you were going to stay for cake?" Barbara responded.

"I was. But Sterling said something intriguing: He believes he can find my friend April Humphry, or at least her body!"

"Her body? Is she dead?"

"Look, Barbara, I'm not sure about any of this, but I'm going to head home. We'll talk later this week, okay?"

"Sure, that's fine. We'll talk then."

"I will. I promise." After a loving embrace, Susan drove home.

She quickly ran to her closet to search for the sweater when she arrived home. After opening several boxes she kept at the top of the shelf, she finally found the pink sweater that once belonged to April.

Changing out of her clothes, she got comfortable. Several hours went by, and shortly before ten o'clock her phone rang. *Finally*, she thought, answering the phone.

"Hello, Sterling?"

"Yes, Susan, hello, I've been giving this much thought, and I'm not sure you're ready to confront the type of criminal we may encounter."

"Don't worry about me, Sterling. I'm tough as nails. Just tell me where to meet you."

"All right, if you're sure, come tomorrow around noon to 410 East Forty-Third Street in New York City."

Jotting down the address, Susan said, "Sure, I'll be there. See you then."

After hanging up the phone, she went to bed feeling anxious. What monsters might she encounter? Regardless, she would finally discover what happened to her friend

Susan had never believed that April left her family without saying goodbye; that wasn't like her. It was an opinion she argued with the local sheriff but he didn't see it that way. She and April had a reputation; they were well known around town as two hell-raisers. Nonetheless, it's time to discover the truth.

Leaving her house shortly past ten o'clock that morning, the traffic entering the city was light. She soon arrived at 410 East Forty-Third Street. Looking about, she could see this part of the city was rundown, a forgotten place people rarely visited.

Walking up to the front of the building, she remembered

Barbara telling her about this place. It was here where Barbara met Sterling for the first time. Barbara said to her that she waited the entire day for the mysterious man to appear, and when she found out he had played a bum and been sitting next to her for hours, she was shocked and somewhat disturbed. Why couldn't they just come out and introduce themselves, instead of choosing to play a foolish charade?

Walking up the stone steps, Susan was surprised that the city hadn't condemned the place. But there it was: a piece of forgotten Americana. Walking through the door she discovered a long hallway with several doors leading to a series of offices, only one with a light inside. There she saw a partition, an iron cage with a small opening. Beside it a door was open to the back offices. Approaching the door Susan twisted the doorknob and walked in.

"Susan Bernstein, I'm in the back. Please join me."

Susan turned the corner and saw an olive-colored man dressed in a silky white Middle Eastern outfit. Atop his head he wore a black turban. Around his neck were decorative beads; leather sandals were on his feet. When the stranger saw Susan, he bowed with his hands held together across his chest.

"Susan, please follow me. You've been expected," the man said, his voice soft and inviting.

Leaving the small office area, the man turned and locked the door tightly behind them. They passed through a narrow hallway that led to a series of rooms filled with old boxes and office furniture. The offices themselves looked as if they hadn't been used in years. They were covered in dust, and desks and chairs sat vacantly, devoid of human contact.

They came to a solid brick wall in the middle of an elaborately carved red metal door. Its brass hinges and sizeable lock meant nothing was getting inside unless invited. The design of the doorway looked like it was taken from an old castle.

The man slowly walked up to the door and took out several keys. He separated the biggest key from the rest, unlocked the door, and pushed it open. On the other side was a massive room decorated with attractive Persian carpets; tapestries hung throughout. The ceiling rose to over forty feet high.

The room was decorated with many ferns and other plants in massive pots near the columns. The smell of burning incense filled Susan's nostrils with the pleasant aroma of cinnamon and blooming flowers.

Looking up, Susan saw heavy wooden beams supporting the ceiling. Decorative, frosted windows were placed between the rafters, allowing filtered light to enter the cavernous space.

In another room Susan could hear distant chanting. Following her guide there, she saw Sterling dressed all in black silk, an outfit that resembled men's pajamas. Around him three Middle Eastern women played small instruments. The song they sang seemed soft and soothing. They were all dressed in white and wore decorative gold headpieces. Their long-hanging earrings were decorated with bright diamonds that sparkled as they moved, and charms dangled from chains at their necks.

Sterling motioned Susan to join him, sitting on a rug with his legs crossed. Seeing her gripping something in a paper bag, he said, "I see you brought the sweater."

"Yes, of course."

Looking at his servant Sterling motioned for him to bring Susan some cushions. A moment later, getting comfortable on the overstuffed pillows, Susan handed April's sweater to Sterling.

"I hope you can find my friend. She deserves more than she got."

"Susan, I've been in constant meditation since we last

spoke. I hope that I've cleared my mind and senses enough that I can see what happened to your friend. I must warn you: What I uncover could be disturbing to hear."

"I don't care, Sterling. Don't worry about me. I'm not afraid so go ahead and do what you do."

Clapping his hands together suddenly, the girls ceased their playing. Setting down their musical instruments, they joined hands and began chanting a low, almost inaudible, mantra. Simultaneously, the servant, standing near, walked toward the adjacent wall and punched a code into a control pad. The windows began to change; somehow the light reflecting properties inside the glass changed, causing the windows to darken. Now only a soft glow from burning candles showed about the room.

All this show seemed ridiculous to Susan. But this was Sterling's world, not hers. The mysterious and enigmatic meant nothing to her. She was a simple gal who was content to work and attend to her garden. Sterling held the sweater in his hands and closed his eyes to all outside influences. Sitting quietly, Susan looked on with great anticipation. Finally, she would know the truth; eventually, the past would catch up with the present.

STERLING WAS SOON TAKEN to a small country setting, with miles of cornfields all around. White houses and barns stretched as far as the eye could see and decorated the rolling hills. An array of bright, colorful lights lit the night sky in the distance. From far away melodies were playing, and people were laughing. Distant screams from kids riding the rollercoaster and Ferris wheel inside the carnival penetrated the silence. The circus was in town. However, the time looked much earlier than now. Several old cars were parked on the grassy clearing, and some slowly left the amusement area.

Sterling's attention was drawn toward the voice of a girl

arguing with a man. As he concentrated on the two, he could hear the man saying, "Come on, toots, have one more drink. It won't kill you."

"No, I shouldn't have drunk the last one. I feel strange."

"Trust me, Babe. You'll be all right. Now kiss me."

"No, I don't want to. I'm going home. Get out of my way!"

Sterling focused on the scene before him just in time to see the tattooed carney say, "No, you're not going home, you tease." He slapped the girl across her face, sending her to the ground crying.

What happened next was disturbing to watch. Sterling shuddered in response to seeing the girl raped. Afterward, she sat upon the grassy knoll, crying, her clothes ripped. The guy buttoned his jeans and shouted, "Now you're a woman. Quit your blubbering, you bitch, or else!"

"I'm going to tell my father, Walter Humphry, what you did to me. Do you think you've gotten away with raping me? No, you are sadly mistaken, you bastard. I promise you you'll go to prison for what you've done. Tell me, do you know what they do to a rapist in prison?"

The scene suddenly changed with a flash of light, and Sterling saw the man placing a series of small stones upon a shallow grave. He moved three much larger rocks in place; afterward, wiping the sweat from his brow, Sterling could see a long tattoo of a dragon running across his wrist, curling around his forearm, past his elbow. The killer left the scene, walked down the hill, passed the security guard locking the gate, and disappeared.

Channeling his powers of observation toward the murderer, Sterling again found himself in another gruesome scene. This time the girl was already deceased. She wore nothing but her bra and underwear and was haphazardly tossed into a shallow grave near a busy road. The scene changed again, and another vision yielded another body. The location was different; it looked to be in a park, next to the bathrooms, adjacent to the small pond. Inside the drainage pipe, weighed down with rocks, the murderer placed a girl's body.

Gratefully, the next scene opened up before Sterling of the tattooed man behind bars. Three Hispanic men beat the murderer severely before the guards came racing in to stop the attacks in a place that looked like the laundry room.

Next, Sterling saw the man sitting in a wheelchair; he looked old and broken. Still, behind bars, it looked as though the man was waiting for the angel of death to appear. Something that Sterling immediately noticed was the fading dragon tattoo upon his arm—a sure sign this was the serial murderer. The man's jumpsuit read Sing Sing Correctional Facility.

Waking up, Sterling opened his eyes. "I know where April's body is located."

"Tell me quickly, Sterling. Where is she?"

"Susan, tell me, what is the last thing you remember about your friend?"

"I awoke not feeling well and told April I was going home. At the time she seemed disappointed. The circus was in town, and she tried to convince me to go, despite not feeling well. All I remember is that we were fooling around at her house, playing outside with her horses. We left one another in a bad way. I never forgave myself; I should have gone to the circus with her."

"I can't say if things would have been different if you had gone. However, I was able to have a good look at her...murderer." His words unexpectedly stuck in his throat.

"I'm not surprised by your comments, Sterling. I initially suspected something like this. It was the only plausible answer to her disappearance. So let me ask, when are we leaving?"

"What? Wait a minute. I never said anything about you

and me catching the killer, did I? First and foremost, I need to contact my detective friend Jack. I need to tell him what I've discovered."

Suddenly, Susan's demeanor changed, and she sternly looked back at Sterling.

"You hold on a minute, young man. Don't you think for a New York minute that I'm not going to be a part of this."

"Susan, no, I never imagined you not being part of this; after all, you're the reason we found your friend. But then again, Jack might have something to say about you confronting this killer. That's all I'm saying."

"Fine, why even come?"

Sterling grabbed ahold of her hand. "Susan, I could have never discovered April's whereabouts without your help. Now it's time we let the experts do their job."

"I suppose you're right, Sterling. Just do me a favor. Will you please hurry and bring April Humphry home? She's been away far too long."

"I understand, Susan. I promise you that April will have justice."

"Good, you made me a promise. I have no reason to doubt you."

Standing, Susan left Sterling's beautiful retreat. Once she arrived home she broke down, crying for her friend. It seemed that lately her life was filled with tragedy. Maybe now all of that was about to change.

Several days later, waiting inside an integration room within the prison, an older man, who looked to be in his seventies, was rolled into the room. From his wheelchair the prisoner scowled at his visitors. He suspected they were investigators, wanting to charge him for some new crime he hadn't committed. The guard, pushing him up to the steel table, locked the wheelchair in place. Afterward, the same guard stood against the wall, waiting.

Jack stepped forward, depositing a crime folder on the

desk with a thud.

"You've been a busy man, Mr. Dixon. Inside the folder is a list of missing young women you have murdered. If it wasn't for the fact that you got busted for bank robbery, I imagine that the list of dead women would be longer than it is. Today with new crime DNA specialists, we can place you at each location of each dead woman's body. This time you'll get the lethal injection, pal."

The man, who cared little for life, heard a smug growling. To him, his past meant nothing, nor did the lives of the young women he'd murdered.

"Listen, cop, you have nothing on me. You only think you do because you can't solve these crimes. Now some dumb-ass crime lab employee has mistakenly placed me at these crime scenes. I warn you that I have a good attorney; you can't pin that shit on me."

Sterling placed his hands on the table. "I saw what you did to April Humphry. Unfortunately for you, we discovered her body where you left it and the other two young women you murdered. Each had lives that you cut short, you son of a bitch. The district attorney has agreed to open these cases. There is no escaping justice, my friend. You're going to pay for the lives you've taken."

Dixon was quiet. His lips smacked together as he pondered the charges against him. He looked back at Sterling; his demeanor hadn't changed. Sterling saw hollow and uncaring black eyes that held no regret.

Nothing would change the man's attitude.

Sterling turned to Jack and said, "We're done."

TIME MARCHES FORWARD, and we cannot change it—no matter how hard we wish. Months later Susan sat in her tiny kitchen alone. She read the newspaper while sipping her morning coffee. The headline read: "Serial Murderer Executed." As she eagerly read the article, it described the last moments of Mr. Dixon's life.

The report described him observing his accusers with hatred while being injected with a solution to stop his heart. He died without regret for his actions, leaving the world a better place.

Susan closed the paper. *Finally, April gets justice!*

Later that day she drove to a small cemetery to meet Sterling. When she got out of her car, she asked, "Are you ready?"

Sterling gave a single nod of his head and followed her to a solitary grave. Susan knelt upon the warm grass near the grave and tried to speak. But the words left her, and she began to weep. She brought some flowers and placed them near the marker, which read April Humphry.

Sterling hugged her warmly as she fell apart. After all these years April was home. That afternoon Sterling heard many stories of their friendship. But, to Susan, a chapter in her life had ended. The mystery of what happened to April Humphry is now solved.

Chapter 5
Achilles

Jack was called to a home located outside the city. There was a murder; that was all he knew, just a death. Arriving at Crockford Lane, Jack parked behind a patrol car. A young boy, around thirteen years of age, was sitting in the back seat. Paramedics attended to the other family members: two young girls; one looked around age ten, the other seven. The mother stood nearby smoking a cigarette, looking nervous.

Jack stopped short, near the yellow barrier tape, and talked to one of the officers nicknamed Smitty.

"So give me the rundown."

"Well, Lieutenant, the young boy admitted to murdering his stepfather. According to the boy, the stepfather was abusing his mother—you know the same old story we've heard a thousand times before."

"All right, I'll go look at the crime scene. Anything else I ought to know?"

"Well, there is something else. The boy, who calls himself Achilles, seems involved in Devil worship or some strange mumbo jumbo stuff. We discovered posters depicting human sacrifices to some devil god inside his room. Besides that, we found various books on the occult and magic, which the adolescent checked out from his school library. The kid also listens to some heavy dark rock music, as evidenced by the record player he had in his room."

"So young and impressionable. There must be someone influencing him."

"Yeah, perhaps. I can't say, but then there is the matter of the murder weapon."

"Okay, I'm listening."

"The murder weapon was a long blade, resembling a medieval dagger, complete with a dragon carved around the handle."

"Tell me, what about the mother? What's her role in all this?"

"I've been able to ascertain she is the real victim in all this. Three years ago she remarried. All the children are from a previous marriage. The boy was worried not only for his mother but also for his two younger sisters. The stepfather had recently shown both the girls special attention. He would take them on long car rides where no one else was allowed to come."

"All right, I'm getting it now."

"Hey Lieutenant, I see the press have arrived. What do you want me to do?"

"Just keep them away long enough so I can investigate the crime scene before they stick their damn noses into the mix."

"Sure thing."

Leaving Smitty behind to deal with the press, Jack lifted the yellow tape and entered the house. The stepfather's body was inside the living room, lying on the floor near the couch. Nearby was a blood-stained sofa where the man had the knife jabbed in his throat. From what Jack could tell, the man had stood to his feet and could only take a few steps before succumbing to blood loss and death.

Atop the man's face was a black silk handkerchief. The material had strange symbols drawn on the surface. It lay over the man's eyes, covered in blood. Searching the entire house for clues, Jack found the boy's room precisely as Smitty described. Posters decorated the walls with dark images of magic. Immediately, Jack knew what he must do. Grabbing his cell phone, he called his friend Sterling.

After a few rings Jack heard a man's voice: "Hello, Jack, what's up?"

"Hey, Sterling, first of all I'm sorry I missed your birthday party. I intended on coming but got called away to investigate a murder. The life of a detective, you understand."

"Jack, did you even read the announcement? It was not a birthday party, as you describe it, but a celebration of a man's tri-quarter event in life in which he fulfills his place in the natural realm of the universe."

"Yeah, like I said, sorry, I missed your party. Look! I have this situation that I believe you would find interesting. It seems that this young boy killed his stepfather with a ceremonial dagger. Besides this weapon I found a cloth across the victim's face with all types of strange symbols, like the stuff you told me about when you were working on the Bishop-Harding case."

"All right," Sterling responded with a sigh. "I'll meet you at the station in a couple of hours."

Closing his cell phone, Jack returned outside to talk with the family. When he reached the ambulance, he looked at the teenager's mother and said, "Hello, my name is Detective Danbury, ma'am. What can you tell me about what happened to your husband?"

Talking a long draw from her cigarette, the woman exhaled the smoke into the night air. "We all went to bed around nine. Sometime around eleven I realized that Ronny hadn't come to bed. It was unusual for Ronny unless he was drinking and fell asleep in his chair."

"Yes, go on."

"Anyway, when I got up to search for my husband, I found my son, Danny; I'm sorry, I mean 'Achilles.' Still, I don't know why he has chosen that name. Anyway, Achilles was kneeling by Ronny's body, holding his sharp knife. In the past I have caught him sharpening that thing as if he was going to war."

"Okay, that's all I need for now. Please don't leave town. I may need to contact you in the future."

"What about my son? What's going to happen to him?"

"He'll be held at the juvenile detention center until a judge sees him. Afterward, I imagine he'll stand trial for murder."

"Murder! I never considered Danny a killer! He's much too young."

"I'm sorry, ma'am, but it's not looking good for young Achilles."

"Oh my god, my son a murderer."

Hearing this, the two girls, seeing their mother distraught, ran to her side and cried out, "Not Achilles. He was trying to save us from our stepfather."

Afterward, they all held one other as if alone in this world.

The truth was that they were alone. The case went to trial some months later. It was eventually discovered that the stepfather was sexually abusing the oldest daughter. Unfortunately, this fact helped little in Achilles's criminal trial. He was sentenced to spend the next twenty years behind bars.

That would have been the future for most killers. Although the circumstances amounting to murder were admirable, taking the law into his own hands could not be overlooked. No, for most a life in prison is the result.

A few months after he was sentenced while sitting alone on a bench in the juvenile detention yard. Achilles was notified that he had two visitors. He assumed they were lawyers from his defense team, asking more questions as they sought an appeal in his case.

Arriving at the visitor's center, he was greeted by two men. One man was overweight, dressed in a Middle Eastern garment. The other man was dressed in an expensive Armani suit.

Achilles sat down. He said nothing but stared uncaringly.

"Good morning, Danny," said Sterling who the well-dressed man seeing the boy for the first time. "I realize we have never met but I want you to know that we have a mutual friend who has nothing but your best interest at heart. Today I have brought someone of great importance who is sympatric toward your cause."

"My name is not Danny; you must have me confused with someone else. I'm sorry. My name is Achilles."

"Yes, fine, if you prefer Achilles. My name is Sterling, not Mr. Sterling, just Sterling. We wanted to ask you about the black cloth the police found covering your stepfather's face."

"You mean that devil that was hurting my sisters? He's dead; I murdered him."

The man sitting next to Sterling spoke up. "I'm sorry, young man, but you did not kill your stepfather. Your sister plunged the dagger into his throat. You cast the spell that kept him pinned to the floor, allowing him to bleed out. I know the truth."

Jumping to his feet, Achilles stepped back, knocking his chair to the ground. "No, you're wrong. I killed that creep! I did it, not my sister Sherry!" The young boy broke out in tears, confronted with the truth of what he was hiding and the fear of his sister going to jail.

Seeing the boy upset, Sterling responded, "Please sit down. Listen to me, Achilles, we're not here to lock your sister away; quite the opposite! Please let me explain."

Rubbing his eyes, Achilles came close to the table, his nose sniffling, "What do you want then?"

"Please sit down. I don't want anyone else to hear what I'm about to tell you. Please sit down," Sterling instructed the boy.

Lifting the chair upright, Achilles again sat down, looking across the table at the two men. "How do I know you're not a couple of weirdos?"

"As I have already told you, my name is Sterling. I'm a psychic detective. I have seen the events leading to your stepfather's death. I know the reason he died. But what's not known is your use of magic. How did you perform the spell? Who has taught you?"

"The truth? I don't know you; I don't trust you guys. My mother has told me never to trust strangers. They will take everything from you and leave you with nothing."

Stannis, the man Sterling had brought with him, waved his hands while saying a spell: "Gormo, Turlingly, Borshes,"

Suddenly, a bluish umbrella covered everyone around the table. Pointing his finger at Achilles, Stannis spoke other strange words: "Susianny, Cising, Zxtex."

Immediately, Achilles was levitated above the floor; at this point Sterling became sympathetic to the boy's reasons for his mistrust.

"What's happening?" Achilles screamed, gripping his seat, not wanting to fall to the ground.

Stannis, finding the situation humorous, began laughing. Sterling, seeing the harmless use of pure magic, smiled. He knew the boy was in no danger and watched Achilles levitate from the floor.

Stannis snapped his fingers and slowly lowered his

hands, causing the boy to descend back to earth. The guard in the room continued to look about somewhat bored, never noticing what had happened.

Sterling repeated the question. "Who taught you magic?"

After Achilles returned to solid ground, he quickly looked under his chair, thinking a parlor trick had been played on him. Seeing nothing underneath except blank space, he looked back at the strangers.

"I heard about a magic store not far from my home. One summer day while my sisters were visiting our Aunt Erma, I boarded a bus downtown to The Magic of the Black Arts store. When I went inside I was amazed to see all the strange things for sale. A guy a little older than me was working behind the counter. I explained the problem I was having with my stepfather and my worries that my sisters were being molested. The guy understood and wanted to help. I told him I had no money but that didn't matter.

"Tell me, Achilles, was his name David?"

"Yes, I believe so. Yeah, that sounds right."

Sterling told Stannis, "David was Shakira's apprentice who works at the magic store."

"I'm familiar with David," Stannis announced. "What I find troubling is the fact that David would allow this agnostic to be exposed to powerful magic—that is unless he was convinced that Achilles had unique abilities worthy of the magical blessing."

Achilles's expression changed. Staring back at everyone, feeling desperate to understand what he was hearing, he leaned forward and said, "A blessing? All I know is that this David guy helped me out. At first I was scared to accept his help. But after he explained that if I wanted to save my sisters, there was just one way."

"Go on, Achilles, I'm listening," Stannis announced.

"Well, I followed David to the basement of the store.

There I saw all kinds of weird stuff."

First, he told them they had walked over to a tall cabinet, and David pulled out an old-looking book and admitted that he wasn't sure how to perform this particular spell.

"He said he was still training," Achilles explained.

Regardless, David told him it was essential that they try the spell. David opened the book and turned to a specific page.

"He told me some lady's name. What was it again? The name of the lady who owned the store?"

Stannis eyed the boy carefully to perceive if he really did not remember the name. "Her name was Shakira, a powerful Spell Builder. She was killed while fighting against a Dark Wizard, whose name I refuse to speak."

"Well, this David guy told me that the last time the book was opened was when Shakira had used it to teach him a magical lesson."

"I'm not surprised," Sterling responded.

"David told me to sit in a weird-looking old chair. He said some strange words to me; nothing happened. Later he asked me if I had a knife or other weapon. I told him that yes, I did; I wasn't about to go downtown without something to protect myself."

"That's understandable," Sterling said.

When I showed him my knife, he held it in his hand and said more strange words. Then he took a black handkerchief from the book with all the peculiar-looking circles and handed it to me. He said, 'When the time is right, take your knife and stab the fabric.' That's all that was needed, he said. The two would ignite together in a magical spell to make my opponent powerless."

"A simple spell of submission," Stannis explained.

"That afternoon my sister Sherry found the knife and handkerchief in my room. She asked me what it was; I remembered David warning me not to tell anyone about the magic or else someone could get hurt. But my sister kept asking me and wouldn't shut up about it. Finally, I told her."

"You must understand, Achilles, no one must know about any of this!" Stannis explained.

Shaking his head in agreement, Achilles continued, "Sherry just wouldn't shut up about the knife. The more I told her to keep it a secret, the more she wanted to know how to use it. My sister needed my stepfather to stop.

"One night Sherry came into my room, crying her eyes out. I tried to calm her down, but she kept saying she wanted to kill Steve. I agreed to tell Mom about the abuse in the morning. But later I could hear my stepfather snoring down on the sofa. Then my sister asked me for a drink of water. She said that she was feeling better. I went to the kitchen, and when I got back upstairs, there in the hallway, I saw Sherry standing next to Steve. His body was lying on the floor, with my knife in his throat. Steve was still moving—until Sherry placed the handkerchief over his eyes. All at once he stopped moving. I was scared of what they'd do to my sister. I yelled at her to go to bed and said I would take care of everything."

Sterling looked at Stannis, his expression one of surprise.

Ignoring the strange stare, Stannis said, "Listen, Achilles, no one has to know the truth. The truth is usually abstractly based on conjecture, simply an opinion based on what we perceive as truth. To society, you are a murderer and nothing more. Here is where you shall rot for the next twenty years."

Achilles stepped forward. "Yes, I took the blame for my sister Sherry; I would do it again! Wouldn't any of you? If your sister was being molested, wouldn't you do the same if not worse?"

Stannis laughed aloud and said, "You're a feisty little rascal, are you not? Nevertheless, we shall allow you this misstep because of your ignorance toward those you address. Listen—don't talk—listen. What I said was society's interpretation of you as an individual—merely a callous killer, ready for the executioner. No one knows of the magical blessing. Be grateful, very grateful, that David bestowed the blessing upon you, young Achilles. It alone is why you're not going to face all those years behind bars, allowing the desperate and heartless killers to have their way with you. Your life, young man, is about to change; you will experience change never imagined. You are about to be reborn, young Achilles."

Stannis stood to his feet and ordered the guard to escort them away. Their visit was over.

Several months later Achilles had a new trial. His defense was an insanity plea. He was ordered to spend the next twenty years of his life at a private psychological treatment facility in upstate New York. The principle administrator in charge was none other than the esteemed doctor named Herbert Stannis.

While Achilles served his prison time for his sister, Sherry continuously visited him. Over the years she never forgave herself for allowing her only brother to serve time behind bars for a crime she committed.

Many years later after Sherry's death Achilles wanted to clear his name. He had another trial. The jury saw things differently, and he was released from prison.

However, the prison had never really been a prison. Stannis made sure Achilles was sent to a school for gifted sorcerers. Achilles became a prized pupil. And one day many decades later Stannis found himself fighting against a new evil born from an ancient horror. Standing beside Stannis was his young gifted protégé—Achilles, a master of the magical arts and spells.

Chapter 6
The Avenging Oath

Sterling arrived at his penthouse apartment, took a shower, changed into black silk pajamas, and then, wanting nothing other than to have a quiet night at home, retired to his living room and flicked on the television, hoping to catch the nightly news. Later after taking a seat in his ergonomic reclining chair he leaned backward, closed his eyes, and shut off his awareness of the world around him.

In the distance he heard a news anchor reading a prepared statement describing the death of a young girl at a place named Union Station.

Sterling began paying careful attention to the story, his interest piqued as he heard the news anchor describe more details about the murder. The Miller family had an adopted daughter who went on a killing spree. Dressed in military armor, she stole her adopted father's rifle and a handgun—he was her first victim. He had just gotten home from his night job and was shot in the head while watching television.

Later that morning, arriving at a red-brick building, the armed girl walked inside. The lobby was full of customers;

she first shot the manager, then a woman working at her desk near the exit. Finally, other patrons, running away to escape the gunfire, were mercilessly gunned down as they raced toward the door.

As Sterling focused he could see the scene opening up as if a curtain had been pulled away. He saw countless bodies in the center of the vestibule. Blood coated the floor a deep red. He heard the loud staccato of an assault rifle firing. Muzzle flashes shone brightly as if a lightning storm was trapped inside the small space.

As Sterling's senses carried him toward the back of the room, a solitary woman, close to thirty in age, stepped out from the other side of a long counter. She wore a red cotton dress decorated with colorful yellow sunflowers. Her red curly hair was tied back with a white silk bow. Her faded freckles and green eyes stared back at him, begging for help.

As Sterling watched several red droplets appeared all over her body without warning. She muttered something that Sterling couldn't make out. Her lips were moving yet he didn't hear any words. A dark figure stepped into view, pointed the rifle at the woman, and began shooting. As her body was mutilated, Sterling screamed.

"What is it?"

"Save us," came a blasting response, as if a loud explosion had struck his apartment building, waking Sterling with fright and causing him to jump out of his chair, panting for breath.

As he came to his senses, he found himself standing in the middle of the living room. A feeling of relief showered him. The entire newscast had been part of his vision. It hadn't happened yet. Thankfully, he wiped his hand across his face. No, he had no control over when an image would appear. However, it would be nice to be able to prepare oneself for seeing a massacre. But there it was. Now where should he begin? This killing spree couldn't be ignored.

His heart was still racing. He stepped out onto the balcony of his flat. It was cloudy and cold, refreshing compared to what had just played out in his head. He could still hear the news anchor describing the events of the murder binge. There are many places with the name Union Station and many people with the name Miller. How to narrow it down?

As he stood at the railing looking down upon the sleepy city, he watched a single car driving down a dark street. Its headlights exposed a row of vehicles parked next to the curb. Where was its final destination? He had no way of knowing but was grateful for the diversion. It would be another sleepless night.

Reflecting on what he had just seen, he tried to recall some unique details of the brick building. Perhaps something could help him identify the location, apart from the ordinary-looking brick exterior found anywhere in this country.

He remembered seeing a series of banners decorating the walls, describing low-interest points, with pictures of families smiling, a series of small offices with glass windows lined the back wall, the walls inside were painted sky-blue, with white trim around the windows, and the floor was newly waxed, giving off bright, shiny reflections of the room.

It was a very average building. There must be something not there or had Sterling missed it? He thought back to the image of the girl. What type of assault rifle was she using? What did she look like, her age, and what was she wearing? These facts were never clear in the vision. It would be so simple to have all the details to help guide him, but that was impossible.

Nonetheless, there should be something in his vision that could tell him the location of the killing spree. It hadn't happened yet. He was sure of that, but there was no time to waste. Sterling went to his computer and searched out names and places called Union Station.

Throughout the country that name was used in shopping malls, barbershops, candy stores—even a few actual train stations. There was even one famous national orphanage that used the term. Something to consider, perhaps? Yes, something to contemplate,

Next, he searched the web for Millers. Of course, it was one of the most common surnames in America. Regardless, the two names together meant something, if only to a pissed-off girl about to commit a massacre.

The long day had its effect upon him. It would be morning soon. Wanting to sleep before the sun appeared, Sterling retired to his bedroom, crawled beneath the sheets, closed his eyes, and tossed and turned.

He had learned something a very long time ago as a way to ignore the mournful cries of the dying. He would first relax his body, imagining himself elsewhere. When the nightmares continued to play out in his mind, he would push away the disturbing thoughts and dream that he was lying in the sand on a deserted beach somewhere in the Pacific Ocean. He imagined the sun beating down upon his half-naked body. He would focus on the sound of the pounding surf, nothing else until the world around him faded into empty darkness, devoid of any noise or disturbances.

THE FOLLOWING DAY HE AWOKE around nine o'clock. Slowly, he crawled out of bed and went about his morning routine. After his shower he shaved and got dressed. Suddenly, he smelled a delicious morning breakfast cooking downstairs. He headed to the kitchen and saw Lucia, his domestic, busily cooking over the stove.

"Good morning, Lucia, whatever are you cooking? It smells wonderful."

"Gracias, Señor Sterling, it's my family's favorite, Huevos Rancheros."

"Is the coffee ready?"

"Si, señor. I received a package from Colombia yesterday. Inside there was the package of your favorite coffee we were expecting. It was a good thing, too. We were running low."

"Thank you, Lucia. I'll have breakfast out on the balcony. it looks to be a pleasant morning."

"Si, Señor Sterling, go sit outside. Breakfast should be ready soon. I'll bring it to you."

"Thank you again, Lucia. What would I do without you?"

"No problema, Señor Sterling. Please take your coffee, and don't forget the newspaper."

"Yes, more news about disasters and political unrest."

Sterling disappeared outside onto the balcony, sat down in a favorite chair, and opened the newspaper. On the front page he saw a story about a robbery at a bank located at First Avenue and Broadway. Disgusted with the bad news, he turned the page to an article about the mayoral election.

Just then a sharp pain radiated from the center of his head. He rubbed the bridge of his nose. A voice cried out in the distance.

"Help!"

Again, he saw the woman dressed in a red, flowery dress. This time more people joined her. Their bloody bodies and lifeless stares looked at him, begging for help. They opened their mouths and screamed in unison.

"Help us."

Their ear-piercing cries were so loud that Sterling found himself holding his hands against his ears, then shouted.

"What can I do? Tell me, where are you?"

Suddenly, opening his eyes to study the hallucination, he saw a red-haired woman holding a newspaper in her hands. "The E....... Gazette" was all that he could make out. The image abruptly vanished. In its place something else appeared. Then everything went black. Two children, a boy and a girl, stood beside their mother crying for their father.

As he came back to reality, he felt his nose dripping blood. A nuisance at best. He took a napkin and cleaned his nose. He looked up and saw Lucia holding his breakfast.

"Are you having one of those visions, Señor Sterling?" Lucia asked.

"Yes, I'm afraid so."

"Señor Sterling, I'm worried about you. Every time you have one of those dreams, it takes you days to recover from the experiences."

"It is my curse in life, Lucia. There is nothing I can do about it."

"Well, I don't like seeing you depressed. Here, eat your eggs before they get cold."

"All right, thank you for your concern. I'll be fine. Would you mind bringing me some aspirin?"

"Si, right away," Lucia replied. "Oh, before I forget, Robin called to ask if you're free for dinner tonight."

"Robin, you say? Sure, I'll call her back sometime this morning. Thank you."

Disappearing back into the kitchen, Lucia returned a few minutes later with a bottle of aspirin and a glass of water.

After breakfast Sterling reached for his phone and dialed Robin's number. He waited for an answer and contemplated their friendship. Though it couldn't be considered a love story and would never amount to marriage, for them it was a relationship with benefits that two grown adults agreed to share. The only caveat to their arrangement came as a promise that if either of them began dating someone new, the other would step away.

After receiving no answer other than Robin's phone recorder greeting, Sterling left a message for Robin to come over for dinner, saying he'd make her favorite: chicken fettuccine.

Sterling spent the rest of the day searching the internet for places called Union Station as he mentally prepared himself for a journey to an unknown destination. He had narrowed things down to the Midwest. Maybe the best thing would be to board a plane and fly to Kansas City. Then, again, he had a superstition about traveling on an aircraft. Instead, he decided it was best to travel by train. *A train*, he thought, *that was odd, even for him*. Regardless, within the hour he made the necessary arrangements. The train route to Kansas City wasn't direct. He would have to make different connections across the United States.

LATER THAT EVENING STERLING was at the stove, busily cooking dinner, when he heard his front door unlock. Peering around the wall, he saw Robin, looking beautiful as ever; under her arm, she carried a bottle of wine.

"Hey, girl, how was your day?"

Kneeling to pet Mr. Wigglesworth, Sterling's cat, Robin responded, "Oh, you know, the life of a prosecuting attorney; some you win, others you lose."

She walked over and planted a kiss on Sterling's cheek. "Dinner smells delicious."

"One of your favorites. Hey, why don't you open that bottle you are carrying, and let's have a glass? You know where the opener is located."

"Sure, can do."

Setting down the bottle, she rummaged through the kitchen drawers, distracted by Mr. Wigglesworth appearing on the kitchen counter, making it known he wanted more loving attention. Robin laughed as Sterling picked up the heavy cat.

"Sterling, did I ever tell you I love your cat? Personally, I don't know why I never got one of my own. But your cat is different; he's a cool cat."

"Good, I'm glad you feel that way. I need to ask you a

favor."

"Sure, yes, go on."

"Tomorrow morning I have to catch a train. I'm not sure how long I'll be gone. If you are available, could you come over and feed Mr. Piggy while I'm away?"

A pause, nothing said, as Robin discovered the bottle opener. Returning to the counter, she gently removed the foil around the cork, twisting the corkscrew into place, then a distinct pop a moment later as the stopper was pulled from the bottle. Taking down two glasses from the cupboard, she slowly filled them halfway. Walking over to Sterling, she handed him the glass, clanked the two classes together, and took a sip.

"You only need to ask. Of course, I'll swing by and feed Mr. Piggy."

"Look, I know it's short notice but I must get on that train tomorrow. It departs early."

Ignoring Sterling's announcement, Robin seemed to be planning something in her head. "Sterling, I have a better proposal: Why don't I stay in your apartment until you get back? After all it's close to the courthouse, and your building is newer than that dump I'm renting. It's a win-win situation; you get a house guest for as long as you need one plus you don't have to worry about Mr. Wigglesworth,"

"It's settled then. Truthfully, there is no one I would trust more. Listen, dinner is almost ready. Would you mind setting the table?"

"Sure, no problem, Sterling. First, tell me, what time do you have to be at the train station in the morning?"

"My train departs at five o'clock. Why?"

"That doesn't give us much time. I have a better suggestion: Let's skip dinner now and focus on the dessert?"

Understanding Robin's meaning, Sterling took his glass and downed the entire contents in a single gulp. Removing the pan from the burner, he set it aside to simmer. Turning to Robin, Sterling smiled.

"I'm waiting on you, lovely."

"Let the fun begin," she announced.

Sterling gave Robin's butt a playful smack as she walked past, murmuring, "Oh, I can't wait,"

STERLING FINISHED SHOWERING at just past four o'clock in the morning and got dressed. He wasn't surprised to smell the coffee brewing in the kitchen. Robin was already dressed, or partly dressed, wearing one of his shirts and drinking coffee.

"Good morning. How did you sleep?" he asked.

"I slept great. Nothing like a romp under the sheets to tucker you out. But, regardless, I have something to ask you. I realize we both agreed to keep our personal lives separate. But because I'm of the female persuasion, I'm curious to know where you're going, especially on a train. Wouldn't it be faster to fly?"

"Ok, but I have to make this quick. I have a train to catch in less than an hour."

"Can I make you some toast before you leave?"

"No, thank you. There's no time. I'm unsure how much time I have before the massacre begins."

"Massacre? Sterling, oh my god, what are you saying?"

"Robin, please don't act surprised. You know I see things, both the strange and bizarre, which can't be explained."

"Yeah, I know about your psychic abilities. But the things you see would scare the shit out of me. So you have a task to complete. I won't hold you up. Give me five minutes, and meet me at my car downstairs. I'll drive you to the train station myself."

"I already called for a cab."

"No, this is too important to wait for a cab. I want to make sure you don't miss that train."

Setting down her coffee cup, she added, "Please don't worry. I promise I'll take care of Mr. Wigglesworth."

Reaching inside her purse, she took out her car keys and handed them to Sterling, then said, "Go warm up my car. I'll be right behind you."

"Okay, sure. Whatever you say. Thank you for everything. I mean that!"

Grabbing his suitcase, he left his apartment and rode the elevator down to the lobby. When he arrived on the street, a yellow cab was waiting. The driver was talking on the phone.

Sterling tapped on the glass. "Excuse me, are you here to pick up a fare for a guy named Sterling?"

Rolling down his window, the taxi driver yelled out, "Yeah, I just called the guy, but some woman answered and told me to cancel the fare,"

"Hey, I'm Sterling. Sorry for the inconvenience. Here, take this, it's fifty bucks. That should cover your cost and more. Thanks anyway."

"Sure thing, buddy. Thanks for nothing." Quickly grabbing the money from Sterling's hand, the taxi drove off in a cloud of dust.

Sterling held up the key fob and hit the unlock button of Robin's car. Just as he was about to start the engine with the remote, Robin appeared.

"Let's get going," she said.

"Sure. Here, take your car keys. Let's go travel to the unknown and mysterious. Where that is, I still don't know."

Robin opened her car's trunk, grabbed Sterling's suitcase from his hand, deposited it inside, and slammed it close.

Standing close to him, she said, "Please listen to me for a minute. You have a calling that no one else can fill. Save the innocent; it is what you do. I have never told you this but I believe in you. Since the Murphy case we have spent a lot of time together, and I have become a believer in your paranormal abilities. You see things that others cannot see. For whatever reason you had a vision of a dreadful slaughter about to happen. Now go and save those people before it's too late and I end up reading about it in the newspaper."

"You will take good care of Mr. Wigglesworth, right?"

"Let's go, Sterling. I would not want you to miss that train."

Leaning close, Sterling confessed, "I don't want to go but I'm afraid I must."

Planting a kiss on his lips, Robin said, "You must go. Who else will save those poor people?"

"No one, I'm sorry to say."

They made it to the train station in record time. Jumping out of the car, Sterling met Robin at the back and grabbed his luggage.

"This is it. I'll keep you posted on what I discover."

Robin watched Sterling disappear from the train station. Returning to her car, she got inside and paused before starting the engine. She thought of the man she had spent the night with and felt a deep, loving affection for him that couldn't be explained. Never a serious relationship between the two, they shared a bond as defenders of the innocent, her through her attorney's office and Sterling through his clairvoyant skills. On a journey. Where? Robin had no way of knowing so she whispered a small prayer on his behalf. It was all she could do besides watch his cat. That cat, why did the feline mean so much to Sterling? This love for his cat, too, seemed a bit of a mystery.

THERE WAS NO FANFARE, NO SAD goodbyes, just the urgent need to catch a train at Grand Central Station. It was a few minutes before five a.m.; although the large locomotive arrived at the station with loud squeaky brakes, no one noticed as they talked busily among themselves.

Sterling followed a group of passengers outside to a

small gate where everyone stood in a single file, waiting to be let onto the platform near the train. An overhead broadcast alerted everyone that the train would soon be boarding. As if on cue a woman dressed in blue opened the gate, and the group walked up the steel steps into the train car.

Sterling asked the porter to direct him to his cabin. As he followed him through the train, most passengers were in their seats, looking anxious to leave. He was careful not to bump into anyone with his small suitcase.

Yesterday Sterling had contacted a lady in Kansas who oversaw social services. The woman, Margaret Toner, agreed to meet with him. She was the head coordinator of the adoption facilities. He arranged a meeting under the guise of being a newspaper reporter from New York. He wrote an article about the adoption train that once traveled from New York, picking up orphans for adoption by families in the Midwest.

After the porter showed Sterling to his private cabin, he quickly changed into his sleepwear, crawled beneath the freshly laundered sheets, and fell asleep. No horrible nightmares or dead bodies, just the blissful sounds of the steel wheels going clickety-clack down the track.

Sterling was startled awake a few hours later, his rest shattered by the continuing announcements coming over the loudspeaker publicizing that breakfast was being served in the dining car.

After Sterling brushed his teeth, he changed into casual wear and left his cabin. As he made his way down the narrow passageway to the dining car, he passed various people sitting in their seats. Some were reading the newspaper; others played with their children. Teens and young adults wore headphones connected to portable CD players, watching their favorite movies and oblivious to the world around them.

Overhead the announcement came again for the nine o'clock seating. Sterling arrived at the dining car, gave his name to the attendant, and waited. A few minutes later he was ushered to a table where three travelers were already eating breakfast. He introduced himself and took a seat. The attendant handed him a menu and asked if he would like coffee.

"Yes, thank you."

After the attendant disappeared a man sitting with his wife introduced himself as Robert Jones, his wife sitting next to him was named Linda.

"Hello, good morning," Sterling replied.

The man sitting next to him took a sip of his coffee and said, "My name is Palmer—Joe Palmer," and stuck out his hand to shake Sterling's.

"How do you do?" Sterling responded and shook his hand in turn.

"Excuse me. Sterling, you said?" Linda asked.

"Yes, that's right."

"Oh, you must try the eggs benedict; the cook knows what he's doing when it comes to poaching eggs. They weren't runny, and the hollandaise sauce is to die for."

"That does sound appealing. I see it's a dish you all must have enjoyed by looking at the empty plates."

"Sterling, earlier Robert and I were discussing the latest politics concerning healthcare reform. What's your stance on these issues?" Palmer said.

Just then the steward brought Sterling his coffee. "Did you decide, sir, what you'll be having for breakfast?"

"Sure, from what I've heard please bring me the eggs benedict."

"Certainly, sir, thank you," the steward replied. Grabbing the menu from Sterling's hand, the man departed.

"So to my question, what is your opinion of today's government?"

Looking up at Joe while stirring creamer into his coffee, Sterling said, "Truthfully, Joe, I don't get into politics or religion—two topics that you can't win. Everyone is entitled to their opinions, and I have mine. It's not worth arguing over, either way." Sterling took a slow sip and set the cup back onto the saucer.

"Please tell me why should an opinion come to an argument? It's just a simple debate between two travelers, nothing more," Joe announced.

"Well, it usually starts that way. But soon everything changes. Something is said that the other party doesn't agree with, and then feelings are hurt. I've seen it a thousand times before."

Suddenly, Sterling felt an emergent perception about Mr. Palmer. The man was hiding something. Then something strange caught his eye. On Joe's left wrist he was wearing handcuffs attached to what looked like a briefcase on his left side. *What in the world are you up to, Joe Palmer?*

"Have it your way, Sterling."

A hush fell over the table.

A few minutes later Linda announced, "Have you ever seen such beauty? Just look at those mountains and the picturesque lake just off in the distance," she said, looking at the Pennsylvania landscape.

"You're right, dear. It's beautiful."

Joe excused himself, saying he must attend to a matter concerning his client's investments, and stood to leave. As he did he gripped the briefcase as if his soul was locked inside. He looked anxious as if he would get caught at something at any moment. Sterling stood to allow him to pass. As Joe moved past the cramped space, Sterling concentrated on the black briefcase to better understand what was locked away inside. He continued looking at it until he heard someone calling his name. Looking over at the sound of the voice, he saw Linda pointing to his coffee.

"Excuse me, Linda, what did you say?"

"Oh, I asked you how you liked your coffee. I noticed they're using Columbian coffee."

"Yes, it is quite pleasing, thank you. Actually, it's all I drink back home."

"So, Sterling, what do you do for a living?" Robert asked.

"I'm a private investigator of sorts."

"Oh, how exciting," Linda exclaimed.

"Yes, quite exciting at times," Sterling agreed, taking another sip of coffee.

Just then Sterling's breakfast arrived.

Robert announced, "Well, dear, are you ready to leave? I want to finish that letter to Jennifer before we reach Parkesburg, Pennsylvania."

"Yes, I suppose. Let me ask: Are you sure you want to mail her that letter? You cannot change her choices for a husband, no more than you can change the weather."

"This David character was recently released from prison; I think it's all wrong. She used to listen to me but now nothing I say matters. I feel she's making a mistake. Come on, let's go!"

"All right, excuse us, Sterling. Matters of the heart, you understand."

"Yes, of course. Before you go I want to say, Robert, I wish you all the best. I mean that, sincerely."

Suddenly left all alone, Sterling enjoyed his breakfast in silence. Precipitously, a steward appeared and began carrying the dirty dishes away. After Sterling finished his meal, he left behind a sizable tip and returned to his cabin. A few hours later he went to the viewing car and found a vacant seat near a window. Sterling had a book he wanted to read called *The Demon Shadow*. As he read the story seemed intriguing, something about the magical world he had a particular interest in studying.

Before he knew it the announcements began saying that lunch was now being served in the dining car. A whole new series of names started being called. Still full from breakfast, Sterling tried to ignore the announcements. But after some time he could not concentrate on his book and decided to spend the next few hours looking out the window instead.

The clicking tracks and gentle rocking soothed him. Before he knew it he had fallen so sound asleep he never noticed the train stopping at their assigned stations on the routes.

As he lay in a deep sleep, an image appeared of a young person running out of a house into the streets of an old, rundown neighborhood. The person's hat flew off their head, releasing long, flowing dark hair. The lone figure wore camouflage and carried a gun.

Sterling could see the road signs—Braxton Street and Thomas Jefferson Avenue—as the person ran past an intersection. He noticed a white two-story house. As he watched what he believed was a girl, she stopped at home and removed something from her coat. A sparking flash from a lighter caused a small flame to appear. She lit what looked like a Molotov cocktail, boldly walked up to the house, and threw the gasoline-filled object at the front living room window.

Flames erupted inside the house. From inside Sterling could hear screams calling to be let free. The girl casually walked to the front door and placed a chain around the door handle, locking it in place. She stood on the street and watched as the house burned.

The girl walked over to the curb and sat down. She began to cry as the flames behind her erupted into a massive fireball. Suddenly, an explosion burst into the night air, tearing apart the entire two-story home. Still, the girl didn't move but cried deeply as if her world had been destroyed.

Sterling jerked awake. Looking about, he discovered

that the train car was deserted except for a young couple making out at the far end and an older woman reading her book. Suddenly aware of the dining room closing announcement, Sterling realized he had slept through the lunch sitting. But it was worth it; he'd discovered a critical clue to the pending nightmare. The streets where the killings would occur are the intersection of Braxton Street and Thomas Jefferson Avenue. There couldn't be many places in the country with such streets intersecting.

Sterling realized his nose was bleeding. As he got older his abilities seemed strained, and the physical aspects of his paranormal dreams affected his body, leaving him with a pounding headache and often a nosebleed. After putting away his handkerchief, Sterling looked about the interior of the moving car. Joe Palmer was sitting by himself, drinking a whiskey on the rocks and looking like he had lost a close friend.

Sterling made his presence known, walking over with a simple "Hello."

"Hey, Sterling," was Joe's short response.

"Do you mind if I join you?"

"No, go ahead and take a seat if you wish."

"Thank you, Joe."

Unaffected by the stranger seated next to him, Joe continued to gaze out into an empty vastness of space.

"Joe, I have met many people in my life, some nice, others cruel and unloving. I can see that you are troubled by something. I'm not sure what it could be but it seems to me that you have done something you regret."

Looking up in surprise, he said, "Why would you say that?"

"Look, Joe, I have certain abilities of observation that allow me to see things that others miss. So when I say something has you bugged, you can bet I know what I'm talking about."

Emptying his glass of whiskey, Joe turned to Sterling.

"Look, pal, I don't know you, and I think we shouldn't speak to one another again. So if you'll excuse me, I'm going to leave."

"It has to do with what you got hidden in your briefcase, doesn't it?"

"Look, Sterling, you're starting to piss me off, dude."

"You stole something that doesn't belong to you. Now you're filled with regret. There's more here that I'm beginning to understand. You decided to leave your family. Start a new life in Costa Rica or someplace? Am I right?"

"How in the hell can you know that?"

"That's not important. What is important is that you're leaving your family to face the disgrace of what you've done all alone."

"No, I'm..." His words trailed off.

"Give it up before it's too late, Joe! Call your boss or whomever you stole from and tell them you've made a mistake. I'm sure that when it's all said and done, you'll get off easy. But if you don't, you'll be running for the rest of your life."

Tears welled up in the man's eyes, and the sudden dark reality of what he's done to his family came crashing into his world—remembering his wife, Peggie, and his children, Robbie and Cathy, back home all alone without him.

Joe pulled out his cell phone and called his frantic wife; she was relieved to discover that he wasn't dead. She had thought the worst—that he had been kidnapped or carjacked. She had been about to call the police. Joe explained slowly, unsure of the response. He was grateful to hear her say that she loved him, no matter what he had done, and that they would get past this as long as they stayed together.

Joe told her he would get off at the next stop and return home. He hung up the cell phone and turned to Sterling.

"This will not be easy. I'll probably spend some time in

jail."

"Joe, please listen to me. When you get home with your family and put your children to bed, look deeply into their eyes and imagine yourself never seeing their smiles again or feeling their loving embrace. Everything in life can be replaced but you can never replace the love of a child that loves you unconditionally. You'll be fine. Trust me, I know."

Grabbing his belongings, Joe staggered as he walked away to get off at the next stop. He hadn't taken less than two steps when Sterling suddenly asked, "So tell me, Joe, what's in the briefcase?"

Holding up the small case, he said, "Oh, this was a way to escape from my troubles. No, I hadn't thought it through entirely but I took what wasn't mine from one of my clients. The man is a millionaire, and I thought he wouldn't miss a few hundred thousand dollars."

"Get home quickly, Joe. I feel that there is still time to make this right."

Seeing the man walk away, Sterling understood that he couldn't see into the man's future. But he knew that no matter what occurred in his life, Joe had a family that loved him. Like a bridge over turbulent waters, they would have each other to face the troubles of the new dawn. In the end what else mattered?

Sterling felt the cold reality that he lived alone become apparent like no other time in his life. He remembered someone he once loved. He quietly whispered her name upon his lips so no one else could hear. "Barbara, I miss you."

Over thirty-five hours later the train arrived at the Kansas City train depot sometime in the morning. Sterling disembarked and stood for a moment. The warm wind felt humid as he looked up at the skyline. He saw the tall skyscrapers of a modern metropolis. Never having visited the city before, he thought it looked pleasant.

Where to begin? The obvious choice would be to search for an intersection in Kansas City where the two names, Braxton Street and Thomas Jefferson Avenue, intersected. Walking away from the train, Sterling followed the crowd of passengers to a large lobby that opened before him. A picture of golden wheat crops on the walls went on for miles. Other pictures decorated the ample space with lone windmills that looked abandoned and broken.

Seeing a sign that read: "Ground Transportation," Sterling lifted the handle on his suitcase upward until it locked in place and walked away toward the rental car agency. Rounding a corner, he saw several small counters where lines of people waited to rent a car. Stopping behind a small family, he stood and waited. After about fifteen minutes the line moved ahead five inches. Looking at his watch in disgust, he thought this would be a long day.

Everyone around him looked weary. The passengers ahead of him looked worn out, probably traveling for days. No, sleeping aboard a train in the long aisles was not a pleasant experience. He was grateful to have arranged a private compartment. Now, bunched up behind tape dividers, they all waited together. Feeling annoyed by the process, Sterling saw the line move another five inches and thought, *at this rate I might have my car by tomorrow!*

After refusing to accept the latest insurance offer, he was shown to an elevator and soon arrived at a vast parking lot filled with various vehicles. Over an hour later he walked up to the counter and gave his information to the clerk. She recorded his data into the computer, ensuring he wasn't a criminal.

Sterling's particular car was located in row B, space 64. He only wanted to get into his car and be on his way by this point. Soon he arrived at space 64. There in front of him was a bright new Cadillac.

Looking the car over for damage and seeing none, he thought, *at least they got that right.* Gripping the key fob, he hit the trunk release and watched the trunk lid slowly open. Depositing his luggage inside, he hit the close button and unlocked the car.

Getting behind the wheel, he plotted the address, Thomas Jefferson Ave. He was astonished to discover not only a street called Thomas Jefferson but a boulevard, road, and drive within the city limits.

The street was where he would start his search. The location was just five miles away. *Good, not too far.* He typed in Braxton Street; a moment later the navigation screen showed the two intersecting only six miles away. Starting the car, he slowly drove out of the rental car garage and arrived at a gate with an attendant sitting inside. He presented his rental agreement to the man and waited.

On the other side of a small office, the man looked up his name and the car type on the computer. Seeing that Sterling checked off the box describing damage to the vehicle, the man handed back the rental agreement and said, "Have a good day, sir, and thank you for renting with us."

Depositing the rental agreement in his glove box, he drove away from the station and quickly came to a stoplight. He glanced about. Everyone was in a hurry as they went about their busy lives in the big metropolis. Sterling thought that if they only knew how their lives were about to be disrupted by the mass shooting news, they might do things differently. Would they stop and take notice? Probably not. Only the loved ones left behind to pick up the pieces would feel the effects.

Just then the traffic signal changed, and he followed a slow procession of cars down the busy boulevard. He soon passed another crowded intersection, grateful the light stayed green long enough to get through to the other side.

After a while he saw Thomas Jefferson Ave. and turned

right. Following it for several blocks, he came upon Braxton Street. Pulling over, he stopped at the curb, shut off the engine, and waited. Not sure of what to expect, he cautiously looked about. Nothing seemed out of the ordinary. Across the street an older man was mowing his lawn. Down the road children were playing in their front yard. Occasionally, a car would pass by, going slow.

Getting out of his car, Sterling stood for a moment. That's when he saw something frightening. There, across the street on the corner, stood the very two-story house he remembered from his vision—the one the girl set on fire. Sitting in the middle of the yard was a For Sale sign.

He gazed up at the property, studying its design. Nothing abnormal, just a house. Why did the murder spree originate here? Or did it? Sterling heard a voice saying something and turned to see the older man who had been busily mowing his lawn a short time ago. The guy stopped and said something Sterling could barely understand over the loud gasoline engine.

The man reached down and shut off the mower. "I'm sorry. I realize now that you couldn't hear me. Can I help you? You look lost."

"No, not really. I've never been to Kansas before. I was just driving down the street and saw the house for sale."

"Oh, you mean the Bentley house? Yes, it's tragic what happened to the young family."

"What do you mean?" Sterling asked.

The man left his yard and introduced himself. "My name is Bob Rogers."

Sterling shook his hand and said, "Hello, I'm Sterling. So tell me, what did you mean about a tragic situation?"

"Oh, well, perhaps I shouldn't say anything. But there was a murder involving the family's little adopted daughter last year. She had an older sister that the family adopted together, obviously thinking that the two would make a welcomed addition to their lonely lives."

"Really, please tell me more."

"Yes, well, I suppose there is nothing wrong with adopting the children of a murderer. The girl's mother shot their father in a fit of rage one night three years ago. She is serving a life sentence as we speak."

Sterling remarked, "I believe I remember reading about that case. You see, I'm a bit of a crime enthusiast. Wasn't there something about the father's affair with another woman?"

"Yeah, something like that. That's how the mother avoided getting a lethal injection—they called it temporary insanity, you understand."

"So tell me about the young girl who died?"

"Oh, you mean, little Annie?"

"Yes, little Annie. What happened to her?"

Bob wiped his brow of sweat and said, "They blamed the older sister. Although they couldn't prove that Isabelle drowned her sister, everyone considered the mother's craziness and thought it was obviously in the family genes."

"Really. So what happened to the girl afterward?"

"Well, she was placed back in foster care. The adopted mother, Brenda Miller, couldn't face the sad reality that Isabelle was a murderer and refused to allow her to stay with her and her husband."

"I'm not sure. But yes, when it comes to murder, there's no clear answer for it. But you'd think that killing your younger sister would seem strange, especially since your sibling was all you had left in your life."

"Not if you were nutty," Bob explained.

"Is this Isabelle nutty, as you said?"

"Well, I'm not sure if she's nutty, but she is strange. Hey, she's now the state's problem. No one in their right mind will ever adopt that girl. Besides, she's fifteen and will soon leave the state's care. Look, Sterling, I got to get back to mowing my lawn."

"Sure, I understand, Bob. Thank you."

Returning to his car, Sterling got inside and drove away. A little later he checked into his hotel. A restaurant at the hotel allowed him to eat his dinner in his room. Afterward he roamed around the hotel and had a cocktail on a patio with a roaring fire pit, and he surmised that nothing else was to be done using his limited abilities. Unfortunately, someone of authority had to be called in to give support. He knew that specific laws were in place to protect children under age eighteen. To tread upon that pathway could be a dangerous proposition. Nevertheless, he must speak to this Isabelle. He felt deep in his soul that she was responsible for the mass killings.

He had to make contact with her. But how? How could an adult man speak to an underage girl and not be considered a creepy pervert? He wouldn't take that chance; too much was at stake. Hearing his cell phone ringing, Sterling swiped the screen. "Hello, Jack."

A FEW DAYS LATER STERLING, Jack, and a local official, Detective Ingram, sat at a cold steel table waiting for the welfare worker to bring Isabelle into a small conference room. While they waited, Jack turned to Sterling.

"You're sure about this, right?"

"I'm telling you nothing in your career has prepared you for this. You had better pay attention to what you're about to hear."

"So what exactly should I expect to hear? This girl was accused of killing her sister, from everything you have said. I've read the report. Although they couldn't prove that she killed Annie, there was evidence that suggests she was the one responsible."

"Jack, that's plain and simple bullshit. Believe me, just wait."

"Just like I've told you over the phone, Jack, our department has reviewed this case, and you're not going to find anything new. The fact is that this Isabelle killed her sister; we just couldn't prove it," Ingram announced.

"We appreciate your time, Detective Ingram, but if you give me a little more, I believe that not only will I prove that Isabelle didn't kill Annie, but you'll discover who did," Sterling replied.

"Let's do this," Jack said, looking down at his watch. "What in the hell is keeping them? I have a plane to catch. I wanted to get back to New York before tomorrow."

The blue faded steel door opened, and a woman appeared, escorting a young girl.

Isabelle was dressed in a plain t-shirt and faded jeans. Her jet-black hair and heavy black mascara gave her a Goth look. She sat at the table across from Sterling, a half-hearted stare that looked more pathetic than defiant.

Her wrists and forearms were covered in cuts that looked to be in various stages of healing. Sterling wasn't sure if they were self-inflicted or the result of fights she had with the other girls or staff at the facility.

The woman who escorted Isabelle stepped forward and said, "These men have a few questions to ask you, Isabelle."

The girl remained silent, saying nothing.

"I wanted to ask you about your sister Annie's death," Sterling, eager to confer with Isabelle, spoke up. "If you don't mind I have some questions I'd like to ask you. My name is Sterling. With me I brought a friend, Jack Danbury."

The girl stood to her feet and turned to walk away. She had only taken a few steps when Sterling cried out.

"Isabelle, I don't believe you killed your sister Annie!"

What happened next came as a complete surprise to everyone in the room. Isabelle turned around and emotionlessly approached Sterling. Without warning she slapped him across his face, then screamed, "Don't you ever mention Annie again, you hear me?"

Immediately, the lady working for the juvenile detention center ran over, grabbed Isabelle, and began dragging her out of the room.

"Wait," Sterling shouted, "please don't take her away."

Isabelle jerked free from the woman's grip and stood firm, not moving.

Rubbing his red, sore cheek, Sterling turned to Isabelle.

"Listen, you don't know me, I get that, and I didn't mean to offend you in any way. In my heart I believe you feel that the whole world is against you. I want you to know that you could not be more wrong."

Turning to the detectives, Sterling said, "I need a moment alone. Would it be possible to talk with Isabelle by myself?"

Detective Ingram said, "What are you saying, alone! You have to be kidding me. I'm about to charge her with assault. Look at your face, man."

After years of experience Jack was never surprised by anything Sterling did. The slap across his face was a small price to allow the girl to vent her frustration.

Turning to his fellow detective, Jack said, "Hey, I have known Sterling for many years, and we have worked on many cases together, solving at least a dozen. Let's leave them alone for a bit. I'm sure he can handle himself if need be. Tell me, where can we get a coffee around here?"

"Sure, why not? It's not like she's getting out of here anytime soon."

The room emptied. With Isabelle alone Sterling remained seated and said, "Would you please come over and have a seat? I want to discuss something with you."

She refused to move from her spot. Isabelle's expression was one of vile hatred. After several intense minutes she demanded, "Why should I talk to you?"

Looking back at her, Sterling said, "Let me ask you: Do

you believe that the dead speak to us?"

"I had a kooky Aunt Alice who believed in that stuff. Personally, I think it's a bunch of crap and not real!"

"Believe me, it's real. I'm living proof," Sterling answered.

Ignoring his comment, Isabelle shouted back, "They blame me for killing my sister."

"Of course they do. Please tell me, who do you believe killed your little sister?"

"I already know who. And when I get out of this place, I'm going to kill them, every last one."

"How do you propose to do that? You're locked away in this facility, and I don't see you getting out of here for quite some time. Do you know another way?"

"I have a boyfriend." She stopped short of saying anything else.

"Isabelle, I want to tell you something. I'm a psychic detective. I know what goes bump in the night. I have seen the other world for myself. In the end don't you want the person who murdered Annie to be brought to justice? Isn't that what we all want, justice?"

"You're beginning to sound like my kooky Aunt Alice."

"I want you to come over and sit next to me. I have something to tell you that I believe you need to hear."

"If you touch me I will scratch your eyes out!"

"Come on, Isabelle, do you believe I traveled from New York to molest you?"

"I trust no one, especially some guy I've never met before."

"Listen to me. I want to catch the ones responsible for your sister's death as much as you do!"

"Why—why do you care? We had never met before! Or could it be that you are some forgotten uncle hiding in the shadows, and now you've arrived to rescue me? If that's true you are a little late, aren't you?"

"I understand you have trust issues. Damn it, who wouldn't? This one time I will ask you to put your mistrust aside and give me a chance to find Annie's killer!"

"Sure, what do I have to lose? I'm not going anywhere, and you sound funny to me."

Isabelle quickly sat down, crossing her arms. She stared back, her expression cold and uncaring. After an awkward silence, then after a bit, she said, "So tell me, what is it that you want me to do?"

"I understand your frustration when it comes to pleading your innocence. No one believes you. This causes a deep-seated resentment that swells up inside you until you finally can't take it anymore and you want to kill everyone you see."

"Yes, how could you know that?"

Ignoring the question, Sterling said, "Please give me your hand. I want to squash all your doubts."

"Oh, I don't know. That's just weird."

"Please tell me what's more important to you, your lack of trust toward strangers or getting the answer on who killed your sister? If we don't investigate this, then I'm afraid your future and the lives of many innocent victims will come to a tragic end."

Grudgingly, Isabelle placed her hands into Sterling's. Holding them gently, he said, "Please close your eyes and concentrate on the last time you saw your sister alive."

The world around him suddenly became dark. Nothing except a blank screen was all that he saw. An eerie silence was all that he heard.

With his eyes still closed, Sterling said, "You must concentrate. I cannot do this without your soul-infused inspiration. You must concentrate on where you last saw Annie."

A short time later, as if a movie projector was turned on, Sterling saw a little girl laughing while holding onto her favorite teddy bear. She wore pink pajamas and was saying something to her older sister. Her words were muffled; nonetheless, she displayed a tender smile, warm and full of love.

Then unexpectedly, Annie's facial expression changed. A sudden frown erased the beautiful smile as a woman entered the room. Sterling guessed it was Brenda Miller. As Sterling watched the woman unexpectedly jerked the young child away and shouted.

"Did you take your bath before you put on those clean pajamas?"

"I don't want to take a bath," Annie argued.

"You're taking a bath, missy. you stink! Now get your little ass into that bathroom or else."

As Sterling watched the argument between Annie and Mrs. Miller, he observed Isabelle saying, "Hey, Brenda, my sister has always had a fear of water. What would it hurt if she skips a bath for just tonight?"

"I don't want any sass from you, young lady. Mind your own business or else I send you back to that adoption agency. You know I have six months to change my mind. I don't care how much money they're paying me. I can always send you back, both you and your brat sister!"

The image unexpectedly changed. Sterling saw Isabelle looking into a steaming hot bathtub. Floating on top, her sister is lying facedown. Screaming her sister's name, she raced over to Annie and pulled her out of the water. Brenda appeared in the bathroom. Seeing Annie in her sister's arms unconscious, she screamed out, "What have you done to your sister?"

Abruptly, the image disappeared. Isabelle ripped her hands free. Tears flowed down her cheeks.

Sterling, seeing her reaction, said, "Now I'm convinced you didn't murder your sister. You loved her too much to harm her, but this Brenda Miller—"

Wiping her eyes across her sleeve, Isabelle said, "That

bitch killed my little sister. I just know it. I'm going to kill that bitch and her whole damn family. You wait."

"There's no need for you to react this way, Isabelle. I have one favor to ask you. Will you allow me time to bring the murderer to justice? Can you do that for me, please? Just give me one week!"

The young girl's expression changed. She looked back at Sterling, considering his request. It was as if plans were already in the works to avenge her sister's death. Now they were disrupted. She had no choice but to agree. Sterling could see through her. She understood that he knew of her plans—he'd have her locked away if she didn't let him help.

There was a missing link, Sterling thought. The undiscovered boyfriend, what part did he play? Would he follow Isabelle's commands or was he the real mastermind?

Both Isabelle and her sister had been left alone to fend for themselves. They had hoped that when the Millers adopted them their lives would turn for the better. But it had all gone wrong. Brenda Miller had been in it only for the money.

"You have one week, Sterling. Otherwise, I will seek out vengeance my way, and it won't be pretty, believe me!"

Leaning close, Sterling said, "You give me a week, and I'll deliver to you the killer of little Annie. You have my word!"

"I'm sorry I slapped you."

"I know you are. Believe me, I knew that would happen."

Looking over at the door, Sterling called out to Jack, and he and the two detectives left the detention center.

A promise was soon satisfied, and Sterling broke down Brenda Miller's defenses using his psychic prowess. She confessed to drowning little Annie in a fit of rage and was later sentenced to spend her life behind bars.

Upon hearing of Brenda's conviction, Isabelle wept

bitterly. Now exonerated she spent several days alone, refusing to speak to anyone.

When Isabelle saw Sterling walk into the room a few days later, she ran to meet him and embraced him tightly. She cried hysterically as she held onto the tall stranger who had given her life a new meaning. At that moment all the hate and bitterness faded from her entirely.

The story broke about Isabelle being wrongfully accused of murder and the foster mother killing Annie. Finally released from custody, Isabelle was happy to discover that she had a distant aunt on her father's side. Aunt Mary soon arrived to bring Isabelle home to live with her and her family. They eagerly took her in as part of the family.

His work complete, Sterling returned to his hotel room. He logged onto the internet and made his reservation for his return trip home—he would fly this time. Afterward he placed a call to Robin to check on things, as he did most nights before going to bed.

On their nightly calls Robin had begun to act differently since mentioning she had gone on a date with one of her colleagues. Intuitively, Sterling probed her until she finally confessed that she liked the guy and planned on seeing him often.

Upon hearing the news Sterling was thrilled that Robin had met someone new. He understood that their friendship had changed and would take a new direction. Although Robin promised to continue feeding Mr. Wigglesworth, she announced that she wouldn't stay at his flat anymore. Again, understandable under the circumstances, he told her.

When they hung up Sterling felt a bittersweet emptiness. No, it wasn't that he had lost a lover, more a close friend. Yes, of course, their friendship would remain intact, and he would stay by her side through the years, even in the saddest of times yet to come.

Years later Sterling received an invitation to Isabelle's

college graduation. Later she let him know she had become a successful lawyer defending the rights of abused children. After several more years passed, Sterling received an invitation to her wedding, then the announcement of her firstborn son a short time later, who she named David Sterling Matthews.

Chapter 7
The Harmsworth Case

It was a sweltering August morning. Sterling had just picked up his double latte and walked toward his car. Suddenly, around the corner appeared a young blonde woman riding a bicycle. Unable to maneuver the sharp turn around a fire hydrant, she ran into Sterling, knocking him down.

Immediately getting off her bike, she ran to see if he was all right. Sterling picked himself up off the sidewalk as the girl began apologizing.

Embarrassed by her fussing, Sterling ignored the pain from his leg and stood to his feet, brushing himself off.

"I cannot tell you how sorry I am. Are you all right?"

"I'm no worse for the wear. Perhaps I'll be a little sore later, but that's it."

"Again, I can't tell you how sorry I am. Please allow me to buy you another coffee."

"No, that won't be necessary. I'm all right."

"I insist you allow me to replace your coffee; it's the least I can do."

Sticking out her hand, she introduced herself. "My name is Molly—Molly Harmsworth."

"Hello, my name is Sterling."

"Listen. I know a place not far from here that makes the best espresso. Let me buy a new coffee. What do you say, Sterling?"

Picking up the empty cup from the sidewalk, Sterling threw it in a nearby trash receptacle and said, "Sounds good to me. Let's go."

A short time later he and Molly were seated in a popular small café. Sterling discovered that Molly had recently become engaged to a young man named Ricky, who was serving overseas. He was due to come home later that month. Molly was studying ancient archeology at Monarch Hill University and was going to the library for her research project when they met. The plan was to have a spring wedding the following year.

Molly was surprised to learn that Sterling knew Professor Etheridge and was eager to hear about how they met until she realized the time and quickly excused herself.

"I must get to the library. Please forgive me."

As she stood to leave, Sterling said with a smile, "Molly, please, no more accidents, okay?"

"I promise I'll be careful. Listen, Sterling, I've enjoyed our conversation. Could we meet again? I promise I won't run over you!"

"It's a deal. See you soon."

From that point on their friendship grew—that is until Ricky returned home. Soon everything changed. Molly wouldn't return his calls and canceled future engagements.

Several months went by without a word. As Sterling busied himself on new cases, he soon forgot about the young girl and went about his life as if they had never met.

One morning as he returned to his favorite coffee bar. In the shadows of the tall skyscrapers a figure waited for him.

"Sterling!"

He turned and recognized the voice coming from Molly Harmsworth.

"Molly, is that you?"

"Yes, Sterling, I'm sorry to bother you but I have this problem."

"Molly, please step into the light so I can see you."

When Molly came into view, what Sterling saw rocked him down to his very soul. The girl he admired for her caring and loving attitude sported a black eye; her bottom lip was split open as though someone hit her in the face.

Sterling gasped immediately, his fist clenched into a ball as he gritted his teeth. "Molly, please don't tell me this was Ricky?"

"Sterling, it's not what you think. Since Ricky returned home he has not been the same. He has these terrible nightmares, and sometimes he gets physical. I cannot tell my parents; you're the only one I know in the city. I don't know what to do, Sterling. I'm pregnant!"

"Oh, Molly, I'm so sorry."

Barely able to move, Molly slumped over while she held onto her stomach. "Sterling, please help me."

Reaching out, he wrapped her arms around Molly. "Yes, of course I'll help you. Tell me, where is Ricky?"

"He said something about meeting a couple of army buddies at O'Malley's Bar, down Third Street."

"All right, Molly, listen to me. This is what we're going to do. I have a doctor friend; first and foremost, I will get you and your baby checked out. Next, please stay at my home to allow Ricky enough time to realize what he has done. Perhaps missing you will cause him to want to seek some counseling. Please listen: This is vital because if he doesn't get a psychological evaluation, he will repeat this abuse until you and your unborn baby are both dead."

"My unborn baby," she remarked as she rubbed her

stomach. "I feel as though something is wrong with my baby."

Looking up at Sterling, she said, "I know you're right, Sterling, but I'm not sure what Ricky will think if I stay at your apartment. When he left me he was pretty upset."

"He's upset, huh? Regardless, tell me his last name."

"His last name is Davis. But, honestly, I don't know what that has to do with anything."

"Molly, I want a doctor to examine you immediately. Can you please allow me to do that much?"

"I suppose it will be all right. Sure, that's okay."

"Fine, come inside. I have some calls to make!"

A short time later Molly was driven to the hospital and seen by a doctor. The news was worse than expected. Molly miscarried, and the damage from the beating Ricky had given her meant she would never be able to have another child. After Molly was given a sedative and fell asleep, Sterling went to chat with Ricky.

Sterling knew he was about to break the law on the way to O'Malley's Bar. When he arrived at the bar, he found the only ones left in the establishment were a small group of men playing pool.

When Sterling appeared in the dingy pool hall, no one paid attention. Maintaining his composure, he walked up to the small group. They stopped playing their game and stood looking at him.

"Excuse me, gentlemen, I need to talk to Ricky Davis."

"Who's asking?" the meanest-looking one in the group responded.

"Tell me, which one of you is Ricky?"

"He isn't here," one of the men answered.

"Fine. Then perhaps one of you could tell me where I could find the coward."

"Coward, you say? Buddy, those are fighting words. I know Ricky, and he is a friend of mine."

"That all right, Paul. I can fight my own battles, just like we did in Kuwait," said one of the men who stepped away from the pool table. "I'm Ricky Davis. Who in the hell do you think you are by calling me a coward? I've never met you."

"My name is Sterling. I'm a friend of Molly's."

"Oh, I get it now. You're the guy that was trying to steal my girl. Yeah, she told me about you and how nice you were to her while I was gone overseas. You were trying to make it with my woman."

Looking back at his friends, he stepped back slightly as if preparing himself to take a swing.

Standing firm, Sterling said, "I came here to tell you that Molly is in the hospital, recovering from the beating you gave her. Not only did she lose the baby she was carrying but she was injured badly enough that she will not be able to have children."

"Hey, man, how in the hell do I know the baby was mine? For all I know the baby could have been yours," Ricky announced with a crooked grin.

Sterling had maintained his composure long enough. By telling the man about Molly, he'd hoped he would show some concern toward the girl he was engaged to. But no! Being a big man around his friends, along with drinking with them for hours, was more important.

He swung at Sterling. And soon the sound of crunching bones and screams of pain filled the small space. Suddenly, there was the distinct sound of a round being loaded into the chamber of a shotgun. The bartender, a close friend of the men lying on the floor, ordered Sterling to keep still while calling the police.

Next, the sound of sirens broke the still silence of the night. Sterling was handcuffed and thrown in the back of a police car when it was over. The other men were taken to a local hospital with broken bones, black eyes, and fat lips.

As Sterling sat in his jail cell, filled with anger, the other prisoners around him steered clear of him until sometime in the early morning. Sterling had a visitor.

"Well, this is the last place I expected to find you, pal."

"Hey, Jack, what took you so long?"

"I was asleep in my bed when I got the call."

Turning to the uniformed officer near him, Jack said, "Go ahead and let him out."

A moment later Sterling stood near his friend.

"Listen to me, Jack, I want to report a crime."

"A crime, you say? What about the assault charges from the guys you beat the shit out of last night? They're the victims. Sterling, you need to curb your anger, son."

Following Jack upstairs, Sterling continued. "Jack, please listen. One of the men you described is named Ricky Davis. The man beat up his girlfriend, Jack. She was pregnant and lost the baby because of it."

"Well, she should have filed an assault complaint with the department. This scenario sounds like a domestic problem. we run into them all the time. Believe me, it won't do any good to concern yourself. Not unless the woman is willing to press charges."

"Jack, listen to me, damn it! For once pull your head out of your ass and hear what I'm telling you. The guy sent her to the hospital. Isn't that enough to have him arrested for domestic battery?"

"You see you're getting all excited for nothing. I thought I made myself clear. We can do nothing unless your friend files a complaint against the man who beat her up. Sorry, Sterling, our hands are tied. Besides, you need to seek legal counsel, my friend. I hear the guy plans on suing you."

"Let him try."

"No, I'm afraid you overstepped your bounds this time. Besides, the woman you're speaking of has checked out of the hospital. She and her boyfriend have made up, and all is well."

Stepping close, Sterling grabbed Jack's shoulder. "I asked you, I even begged you, to do something but you refuse. If anything happens to Molly, I hold you responsible, Jack, and you alone."

Brushing his hand away, Jack announced, "Sterling, quit getting so melodramatic. It's a personal matter between the woman and her boyfriend, none of our concern."

"Am I free to leave, Jack?"

"Sure, just don't leave town," Jack said with a chuckle.

Weeks went by and still no word from Molly. When Sterling's arraignment appeared on the calendar, he went to court, hoping to see Molly. Instead, he saw a pompous Ricky and his buddies emerging with their military medals and haughty demeanors. They described to the judge how Sterling appeared that night and took advantage of their drunken state to overpower them.

At hearing this Sterling chuckled aloud and thinking to himself, *Even if they were not drinking, the results would have been the same.* Sterling had a six-degree black belt; they hadn't stood a chance. Regardless, Sterling wanted most to see his friend Molly, but he had no way to get hold of her. Her phone number had been changed, and Ricky had been granted a restraining order against him, which meant there was no way to see her again.

Gratefully, Sterling only received probation. Ricky and his cronies met him as he and his defense attorney left the courthouse.

"Well, big man, you may have gotten off easy. But let me tell you, if ever I see you alone on the street, I'm going to finish this. You haven't heard the last from me."

Jeers came from Ricky's buddies. Sterling wanted another go at the small band but knew it was best to walk away. As he did he heard Ricky.

"Sterling, this isn't over, not by a long shot."

His attorney, Shane O'Connor, immediately grabbed ahold of his coat and said, "Leave it. Come. Now let's walk away."

"Sure, I will. But first, give me a moment!"

Turning back toward the small group. Sterling announced, "I'm here now. Come on. Give me all you got."

The small group shuffled their feet, turned around, and left. That was all over; Sterling hoped to put this Molly thing behind him and go about his life.

Time slowly passed. Soon Sterling's life returned to normal—that is, normal for a psychic detective. One night while sitting in his room meditating on a new case, he focused on the young girl who had gone missing from the playground. One minute her mother was watching her on the swings, the next she was gone.

As Sterling held onto the girl's favorite dolly, he was unexpectedly shaken by the image of Molly arguing with her boyfriend Ricky.

Sterling could see Ricky holding a knife across Molly's throat, threatening to slice her artery if she didn't shut her mouth.

As Sterling watched he saw Ricky suddenly punch Molly in her face. Sterling, troubled by the vision, walked over to a nearby window overlooking the city. His choices were limited. What could he do except wait for the inevitable to happen?

Sterling went to bed that night, frustrated by the vision. It took some time before he was able to fall asleep. Sometime in the early dawn he was awakened by a disturbing feeling that something was wrong. Smelling smoke, he got out of bed and headed for the stairs. There in the living room a fire raged out of control.

He only had one thought: to save Mr. Wigglesworth, his cat. As the fire spread it engulfed his long curtains and expensive tapestries. Soon smoke filled the entire space of his living area. Hearing a noise, he was relieved to see his cat sitting on a high shelf. Grabbing the cat, Sterling began coughing as he searched for the door. The heat was intense. Tucking his cat beneath his shirt, Sterling felt the walls, trying to find the exit to the garage.

As he pushed on the door, something on the other side blocked his escape.

"Damn it," Sterling exclaimed.

He returned to the smoke-filled room, avoiding the rising flames as he went to the front office. The door was locked. Sitting Mr. Wigglesworth down upon an old, abandoned desk, Sterling grabbed hold of one of the old steel chairs, lifted it above his head, and heaved it through the glass window. Grabbing his cat, he ran to the front lobby; again, the exterior door was locked—a chain had been wrapped through the door handle, preventing his escape.

Sterling gave the solid door a karate kick that rocked the frame. Again and again he kicked the door until the hinges that kept it in place began to twist. Relentlessly, he continued his assault until the door split apart.

He ignored the blood that poured from his leg and walked out into the open night air. Coughing repeatably, Sterling set Mr. Wigglesworth down on the cement step. Instantly, the cat ran away but Sterling knew he would return; he was only panicked.

Off in the distance sirens blared. But it was too late to save his home. As he sat watching the firefighters work, something caught his attention. A dark sedan pulled away from the curb, headlights off. A low rider, it had large, chrome spinning wheels. He had seen the same type of wheels on Ricky's car at the courthouse many months before. And a unique, throaty rattle came from the muffler. Sterling whispered, "Ricky, we're not done, not by a long shot. We'll meet again, I promise you!"

WEEKS HAD PASSED SINCE the fire had nearly taken his life. As Sterling drank his coffee, the expression on his face said it all. Alone in the busy coffee shop, near the window in the corner of the room, he remained aloof from any human contact. This place was the coffee house that Molly had initially recommended to him during their first meeting. Now it was a favorite haunt of his.

When the arson detectives finished their investigation, it was discovered that a fire accelerant was used to light his dwelling ablaze, probably gasoline. Sterling had lost many treasures, but he and his cat were spared. When the fire investigators probed him for answers on who set the dwelling ablaze, he remained silent.

Revenge, he thought, *is best served cold.*

Luckily, he had never kept most of his prized processions at home, although he had lost his favorite Porsche 911 Carrera. That was soon replaced by insurance. Now he waited for Jack, who had called and asked to meet with him. Jack wasn't his usually demanding self so he obliged him, even though he was busy. Things between them had become strained since their last conversation about Molly's abuse. Sterling felt in his heart that Jack had enough evidence to lock Ricky away. But why the hesitation? He could never understand!

Yes, Jack insisted that without Molly pressing charges against her fiancé, the police could do nothing to help her. But Sterling knew that the detective had bent the rules in the past. Why should this case be any different?

Jack walked through the coffee shop door, and Sterling noticed a troubled look on his friend's face.

"What are you drinking today?"

"Just the usual black tar, thanks."

Getting the attention of one of the servers, Jack soon had his coffee.

"Listen, Sterling, there's something I need to talk to you

about."

"Yeah, go ahead, Jack. Tell me, what's on your mind?"

"Listen, we have known each other for a long time. I haven't always had the right answers to know what needs to be done. Working in the police force I have seen a lot of murders and morbid stuff. You know this already."

"Jack, I can always tell when you're beating around the bush. What is it? Wait, wait, I sense something, something you're about to tell me is terrible."

"We got a domestic violence call last night. There had been numerous reports of abuse, and it all came to a head last night. A man apparently overreacted when his girlfriend said she was leaving him."

"Molly—are you talking about Molly, Jack?"

"Yes, I'm afraid so. This Ricky character bludgeoned her to death. He claims that he was having a flashback from being over in Kuwait. Regardless, he killed the poor girl. He's now in lockup, behind bars.

"No, no, damn your soul to hell, Jack. I begged you to do something. I hold you responsible, Jack. You should have done something to help Molly."

Tears ran down Sterling's cheeks as he stood to his feet while shaking his fist at his friend, struggling not to take a swing.

"Go ahead. I deserve it. I wouldn't blame you if you did."

"No, Jack, you stupid bastard, you're not getting off with a simple punch across your jaw. We're through, do you hear me? We're through! I never want to talk to you again! Not unless it's a life-threatening emergency. Good luck with your guilt. You could have done something for Molly but refused because of some bullshit law." He took his coat and left, leaving Jack to contemplate his words.

Who knows if a murderer ever feels regret for their actions? Perhaps in human nature one could possibly accept their deeds as something horrible they have caused and feel remorse. In the end murder is murder, but to kill an innocent, a day of reckoning will arrive sooner or later. Ricky Davis had had everything, the love of faithful women, a bright future ahead of them.

Regarding his trial Ricky could only afford a public attorney to defend himself. That was until one day his public defender was unexpectedly dismissed, and a renowned lawyer stepped in to take his case. The charge was murder in the first degree.

Ricky's case was moved forward on the docket. The judge, sympatric toward the army veteran, listened to the arguments coming from the district attorney and chief prosecutor. Ricky Davis was ordered to serve four years in a minimum-security prison, where he was to receive counseling for PTSD. Afterward, he was given probation for seven years.

Time went by quickly. Ricky had gained about thirty pounds on his release from prison. He looked forward to a new life and had met someone online. His outlook for a bright future seemed promising. Forget about what he'd done to Molly; that was in the past, after all. Still, everyone he knew was surprised that he missed his first meeting with his probation officer. Afterward his new girlfriend filed a missing person's report with the police.

Time marches on, and after a couple of weeks his probation officer received a postcard from Honduras, saying that he was never coming back to the United States. He had found happiness in the arms of a beautiful woman. The postcard went on to read: "Tell all my friends goodbye; they'll never see me again."

Yes, some of the words written on that postcard were true. In the end Sterling had his vengeance. No one ever saw Ricky again. His death was not as merciful as he had hoped.

IN ANOTHER PART OF THE WORLD, a tall cliff overlooks the beach below, surrounded by an iron barrier. A solitary gravesite neatly decorated with white marble and gold leaf inscriptions is Molly Harmsworth's final resting place. The sacred site, decorated with an assortment of flowers, is only accessible through a metal gate; only one of Sterling's servants can unlock it.

Next to her lone grave is another. Its white marble headstone reads: "Sterling, Born 1955." Next to it, the word "Died." That particular date is still blank.

Acknowledgments

If I'd been a better listener or perhaps a better student, then possibly I would have gone far in life. But as it is, I'm happy. I want to acknowledge the teachers in my life—all those teachers who struggled with overcrowded classrooms and budget cuts but still fought bravely each day to teach knuckleheads like me. I thank you and applaud your hard work.

About the Author

Timothy Patrick Means was raised on the sunny beaches of Southern California. As a young boy he spent many summers swimming and playing in the ocean. Later he was fortunate enough to land a job in Aerospace, working for McDonnell Douglas. He worked on military aircraft and, most exciting of all, rockets! All types of space hardware, including the space station, space shuttle, and the Delta rocket.

His life has always been interesting—a father to four children and two stepchildren, a grandfather to fourteen. And through it all he has always found time to write. "My first experiences at being creative were describing my feelings through poetry, which I did with mixed results," he explains. But it wasn't until he discovered the fun of writing about the paranormal that his imagination soared, and he "was set free to explore all the possibilities of creating an exciting story."

The Sterling Chronicles is part of the Bishops' Sacrifice Series, a collection of short stories further exploring the adventures of the mysterious psychic detective who is featured in the series. He is also the author of a pirate series called *The Iron Born Pirates*. You can find his work on Vella, on Amazon, and wherever books are sold.

Find out more at: www.timothypatrickmeans.com.

Manufactured by Amazon.ca
Acheson, AB